NO

ROAD

TOO FAR

ENDORSEMENTS

"A TOUR DE FORCE THAT opens our eyes to the truths of God's Word! Like all good biblical fiction, John Kitchen's short stories provide rich insight into the history, culture, and customs of the ancient Middle East. But along with that, they open our hearts to the thoughts and motivations of the characters of Scripture, both those we know and those who are not mentioned. Read these stories for entertainment as well as biblical background, but more importantly for the timeless wisdom that they give."

—David E. Fessenden
author of *The Case of the Exploding Speakeasy*

"IN *NO ROAD TOO FAR,* John Kitchen cleverly and creatively weaves historically believable characters into biblical accounts of Christ, stirring the imagination (and the soul) while remaining faithful to the Scriptures."

—Nathan Birr
author of *The Douglas Files* and *Last Resort* series

ENCOUNTERS WITH THE CHRIST

NO
ROAD
TOO FAR

*No matter where life has
taken you there is no road too far
for God to find you . . .*

JOHN KITCHEN

A COLLECTION OF SEVEN SHORT STORIES

AMBASSADOR INTERNATIONAL
GREENVILLE, SOUTH CAROLINA & BELFAST, NORTHERN IRELAND

www.ambassador-international.com

No Road Too Far: Encounters With the Christ
©2022 by John Kitchen
All rights reserved

ISBN: 978-1-64960-314-2
eISBN: 978-1-64960-336-4
Library of Congress Control Number: 2022947807

This is a work of fiction. Names, characters, and incidents are all products of the author's imagination or are used for fictional purposes. Any resemblance to actual events or persons, living or dead, is entirely coincidental. Any mentioned brand names, places, and trademarks remain the property of their respective owners, bear no association with the author or the publisher, and are used for fictional purposes only.

Cover design by Hannah Linder Designs
Interior typesetting by Dentelle Design

Scripture taken from The Holy Bible, English Standard Version. ESV® Text Edition: 2016. Copyright © 2001 by Crossway Bibles, a publishing ministry of Good News Publishers.

AMBASSADOR INTERNATIONAL
Emerald House
411 University Ridge, Suite B14
Greenville, SC 29601
United States
www.ambassador-international.com

AMBASSADOR BOOKS
The Mount
2 Woodstock Link
Belfast, BT6 8DD
Northern Ireland, United Kingdom
www.ambassadormedia.co.uk

The colophon is a trademark of Ambassador, a Christian publishing company.

to

Jesus Christ

the greatest Storyteller

the hidden character in every story

the center of the one, great Story

CONTENTS

[handwritten annotations:]
Luke w/ patient
midwife
Easter — shepherd who didn't see the host of angels
c/b
Easter
Ethiopian Pentecost
Carpenter
mortise &
Angels remember their role in human history b/c the last battle
Rabbi who told Herod that Bethlehem was where...

NO ROAD TOO FAR

LEFT OUT. LEFT BEHIND. LEFT for dead. Many people feel they have simply gone too far, and all hope is lost. But there is no road too far for God to know you, to love you, to come to you.

Through the moving accounts of individuals who, for various reasons, felt they had gone too far, let's discover for ourselves that there is no road too far for God's love to reach us. In seven stories of biblical fiction, we explore not only the struggle of the hopeless soul, but also the hope offered us by Jesus.

No matter where your road has led you, no matter how long it has been, no matter what you have seen or what you have done, God is coming to you, calling to you, reaching to you. Hear Him crying to you, "There is no road too far for the reach of My love!"

The story of redemption in and through Jesus is true. The stories that follow seek to tell that ever-true story by way of fictionalized renderings of several factual stories conveyed in Scripture. A guide to Scripture references is included at the end of this book with the hopes that you will further explore the facts and hope behind these fictionalized accounts.

STAND UP AND BE COUNTED

HIS HANDKERCHIEF WAS SOAKED THROUGH with crimson stains. The coughing came hard and continued inescapably.

"Please, let me call a doctor!" Floriana begged, exhausted from the long vigil at her husband's side. Breaths were difficult to come by, so, reluctantly, he consented, bobbing his head in a sign of surrender.

An hour later a neighbor reported, "I was unable to locate your doctor, but I happened upon a physician named Luke, who is temporarily detained in town while on a journey with companions. He promised to come as soon as he is able." This news was met with another barrage of hacking gasps for air.

During a respite in their vigil, a distinct rap came at the door. As Floriana threw open the door, her eyes fell on a tallish, middle-aged man with dark features and curly, black hair.

"Peace," he greeted her as he deferentially bowed his head. "My name is Luke. Did someone here call for a doctor?"

Ushered into the humble home, Luke was led to a back room where the patient had been caught in the grip of another violent attack. Luke settled in at the side of the bed and waited for a retreat of the spasms. Finally able to address the patient, he introduced himself and asked about his needs.

The form before him was clearly in desperate shape. Despite advancing age, there remained under sallow skin the fading frame of a once-powerful warrior. A cursory physical exam exposed several long scars, hints at tales of battle waiting to be told.

11

The ravaged form seemed to momentarily increase in strength as the patient announced, "I am Manius Galarius Justinius, a proud soldier of Caesar's Legions."

As quickly as his strength had risen, it faded again under a hail of racking coughs. He brought the handkerchief again to his mouth. The rustle of a crow fleeing its perch outside the window caught the trio's attention. The black specter escaping into the sky somehow seemed ominous.

With a clearing of her throat, Floriana broke the silence, quietly correcting the introduction. "*Retired*, but still proud, soldier of Caesar's Legions."

Luke looked down upon the broken man before him. The hints of a once well-developed frame were being erased by the inevitable approach of death. Upon inquiring, Luke learned that Justin, as he conceded to be called, had settled after his service here in Troas, a Roman colonia that was home to many a retired soldier. A small plot of land and a pittance of a pension was his reward for tramping the breadth of the empire, facing privations of staggering dimensions, and taking his life in his hands time and again in defense of Caesar and the glory of Rome.

"How many years did you serve?" the doctor asked, continuing his assessment. "The standard twenty-five?"

"Yes, twenty-five, and then seven more for good measure."

Trying to remain clinical and unaffected, Luke asked, "What has your personal physician told you of your condition?"

Justin cast a glance at Floriana. When their eyes met, she looked to the floor. Luke followed their nonverbal exchange, and then his eyes met again with Justin's as he burst into another spasm.

Mopping his mouth dry again, Justin said, "A tumor. Somewhere in the lungs."

Now Luke's glance fell to the floor. "And his prognosis?"

Silence. All eyes down. Floriana was the one to finally break the awkward silence. In a soft voice, she whispered, "Incurable."

"A timeframe?"

Justin took up the question. "Impossible to be certain, but less than three months. Perhaps one."

Luke absorbed the news. The cold chill of despair that had settled upon the home now rushed down his own spine.

"I have something here that I have found helpful against an otherwise uncontrollable cough." Turning to Floriana, he asked, "Could you boil some water? I have some herbs that I think will settle the worst of this for the time being."

Floriana spun around and set off to her task.

As Luke searched through his bag, Justin turned the conversation. "So, why are you in town? Something about a journey being delayed?"

Luke quickly tried to assess just how much of this story the patient would be interested in, and, for that matter, be ready for.

"Maybe we shouldn't talk too much," Luke said, "because of your cough."

"Oh, don't worry about it," the soldier answered, waving dismissively. "It's just as bad when I don't talk."

"Well, in that case," Luke said, "yes, I am a part of a team that has traveled the breadth of Asia and are awaiting word about our next steps."

"Awaiting word from whom?"

Again, Luke surveyed Justin, trying to decide how to navigate this conversation. Not confident of the timing, he spun the conversation back upon the retired warrior. Ignoring the question just put to him, he asked, "So, tell me about your service of Rome. Where has it taken you?"

Always ready to unspool a story, Justin's face brightened a bit, and he seemed not to care that his question had gone unanswered.

"Just about everywhere! From Gaul to Judea and everywhere in between."

"What made you sign up?"

"Since I was a boy in Lanuvium, it was all I'd ever wanted."

"Lanuvium? Isn't that near Rome?"

"Yes, a short twenty miles to the southeast. It is the hometown of the illustrious General Quirinius. I relished the stories that filtered home about his heroics. Around fires, the old ones used to spin the tales of Quirinius' desert campaign in Cyrene, of his peace mission in Pisidia, of his conquering the famed mountaineers of the Taurus range, and of his rule in Crete. It was in those nights around the fire that the blood of Rome began to course through my veins and the command of Caesar became an obsession. As soon as I turned twenty, I was at the recruiting station."

"And you enjoyed it so much, you stayed on for thirty-two years?"

"*Enjoyed* is perhaps not the right word."

He erupted again into a fit. Several minutes later, after his chest stopped heaving and he'd caught his breath, he repeated, "*Enjoyed*, as I said, is probably not the word. It was more like a call, I suppose."

"A call?" Luke asked as he raised an eyebrow.

Just then Floriana returned, a steaming kettle in hand. Luke took it from her and set the herbs to steeping.

He turned back to study the proud legionnaire as Justin said, "Yes, I suppose *call* is the right word. It felt like what I was born to do. In the service of Rome, I seemed to find my place. As if guided by an unseen hand, I was where I was supposed to be, doing what I was born to do."

"Not many men can say that."

"No, I suppose not," Justin said as a reflective expression swept over his face.

He paused to assess what he'd just revealed, as if it had never quite occurred to him before. "And you?" he said. "How did you decide to become a physician?"

"I wanted to help people. I wanted to make a difference. I thought medicine would be the best way to do that."

"And has it been?"

"I can't say that I've felt about medicine what you've described about serving Rome. Maybe I am a man with too many interests."

"Such as?"

"History, for one. Medicine is wonderful, don't get me wrong. It does provide an avenue for service, for which I am grateful. But I *love* history."

"Oh! Then I'm your man!" Justin said, seeming to have tapped into a hidden stream of energy. "I can give you details on some of the greatest battles of Rome's past five decades." And so, he launched into dramatic expositions of the blood and guts of defending Rome's glory, stopped only by intermittent rounds of coughing that were held at bay by sips of Luke's herbal brew.

Luke leaned back and decided to give this dying man the gift of a listening ear for a while. Besides, Luke's team wasn't ready to leave yet.

Time slipped away, and the lady of the house appeared again, this time with two bowls of meager soup and a loaf of crusty bread. With a brisk curtsey, she placed it on the roughhewn table at the side of the bed and darted out again.

Luke propped Justin up in bed and got his soup in hand. Then he gathered up his own and paused momentarily, bowing silently. Then he dug in.

"What was that?" the patient asked.

Luke gnawed on a hunk of bread with a quizzical expression.

"What was *that?*" Justin repeated, gesturing in the doctor's direction.

"A prayer," Luke mumbled through a mouthful of dough.

"Ah, a religious man," the once-great soldier exclaimed, not sarcastically, but not sympathetically either.

The presence of the meal only paused Justin's monologue. Between bites and coughs he launched in again.

Luke decided finally to jump in, asking, "Was everyday as glorious as you describe?"

"Oh, no! Tedium's the norm in the army," Justin explained. "You spend ninety-nine percent of your life bored stiff, and one percent panic-stricken, with your life hanging in the balance."

"What's the worst assignment you ever drew?" Luke asked.

"That's an easy one," Justin replied. "Judea."

"Judea? Why Judea?"

"I was just twenty-three. I'd only been in the service of Rome for three years. I spent those three years putting in one transfer request after another. Finally, I was assigned to serve under my hometown hero, Quirinius himself." He paused. "I suppose I thought it would all be like the stories I heard around the fires back home as a kid."

"It was a disappointment?"

"*He* was no disappointment! But my first assignment under him certainly was."

"What was so bad about it?"

"Census work. Counting heads. Absolute, tedious monotony!"

At that, Luke sat up so quickly that he choked on the bread that he was eating. Now he was the one fighting for air! A moment later, he used the first breath to return to his lungs to ask the question, "You were part of the census?"

"Yes," Justin muttered slowly, drawing out the word and wondering what could be so exciting about a census, especially *that* census.

"You were in Judea doing census work? Was it the census ordered by Caesar Augustus about fifty years ago?"

"Yes."

"Oh, my! I can't believe it! This is wonderful!" Luke exclaimed, setting aside his bowl and spoon. "You can help me! *You* can help me!"

Justin clearly was lost, and it showed. So Luke slowed down and tried to explain.

"I told you I love history."

"Yes, we've covered that."

"Well, I am actually writing a history right now. And I need eyewitness testimony about some aspects of that census and how it went down in Judea."

"Okay," Justin said, still uncertain of what could be so interesting about the dullest duty he'd ever pulled. "What do you need?"

"Where were you, precisely?"

"Judea."

"I know, but *where* in Judea?"

"Several places. Mostly backwater villages. Hardly even got to Jerusalem."

"Okay, but *where?*"

"That was half a century ago! I don't recall exactly. The names were strange to me, anyway."

Realizing he was going at this the wrong way, Luke changed his approach. "Were you ever in a place called Bethlehem?"

"Bethlehem?" Justin turned the name over in his mind, scouring the landscape of his memory. After a moment, his eyes brightened a bit, and he asked slowly, "Not too far from Jerusalem?"

"Yes," Luke said, nodding excitedly.

Justin's eyes brightened even further, "A sheepherding community mostly?"

"Yes!" Luke said.

"Nope," Justin said, his face flat and expressionless. "Nope. No, I don't recall a thing."

Luke screwed up his face, his hopes clearly dashed. "No? Nothing at all?" he sputtered.

The corner of Justin's mouth slowly curled upward in a wry expression. Then the other corner joined in the fun, until a broad, impish grin exposed the few teeth he had left. "Yes, of course, I remember! I was just playing with you!"

What started as a chuckle erupted instead into another lung-wrenching coughing fit.

Luke grabbed for the herb concoction. After a few sips, Justin settled back, smiling through the pain and gasps for air.

"Had you going, didn't I, Doc?"

"Yes," Luke replied sheepishly. "Yes, you did. So tell me about it."

"Not much to tell. People. Everywhere people. I don't know what's with those Jews. Unlike every other citizen of the empire, they insisted they could only register in their ancestral hometowns instead of where they actually resided. What a nightmare! The entire province was like an anthill."

He paused, shook his head almost imperceptibly, and took another sip of his herbal mix.

"That's the only reason I was there."

"What do you mean?" Luke asked.

"The Jews have always been a pain in the emperor's backside. There was always something fomenting somewhere in those hills. That's why Augustus asked personally for Quirinius to oversee the census in Judea. After his success in making and keeping peace in Pisidia, he was the emperor's go-to man."

Luke brushed off the stereotypes and said, "There is someone in particular that I'm interested in."

"We counted thousands! Everyone in the entire empire had to stand up and be counted. How am I supposed to remember one person?"

"It was actually a man and a pregnant woman. They traveled down to Bethlehem from Galilee—a place called Nazareth." Luke paused; studying the soldier's face, he looked for any sign of recognition. Seeing none, he added another hint. "Shortly after they arrived, she went into labor. They were lodged with the animals."

"Animals! Why?"

"Like you said, there were people everywhere! There was no room anywhere for them." Luke kept fishing. "On the night of the baby's birth, there was a commotion."

"What kind of commotion?"

"Shepherds—middle of the night. They came telling a tale of angels announcing the baby's birth."

Justin leaned his head back and thought deeply. He chased a ghost of a recollection, but the apparition darted away as soon as he recognized it as a sliver of something real. He shook his head in frustration. He looked up to give Luke his full attention as he broke the bad news; but then, as quickly as it had disappeared, that whisper of a memory danced again on the fringes of his conscious thoughts. His hand went to his mouth again, not to stifle a cough this time but in concentration as he began putting bits and pieces of memory together into a coherent mental picture.

Slowly, softly, he said, "Yes! Yes! I do remember something."

Luke leaned in. "What? What is it?"

"There was some confusion because while they were betrothed, she was pregnant. So, there was talk about that and some confusion on exactly how to enroll them for the census." His eyes darted back and forth without fixing upon anything in particular, his mind grinding out the shards of memory. "And, yes, I do recall something about those shepherds. Said something about the child being a Savior, and they called him Lord. I warned them to watch that talk. Those are titles that belong only to Caesar, and if he or one of his loyalists caught wind of it, it could be the end of the baby. As I recall, his parents named him Jesus.

"Isn't that weird?" Justin asked, shaking his head with a smile on his face.

"What?" asked Luke.

"Oh, that I'd remember them. After half a century, after thousands of miles, after multiple thousands of people, I remember *them*." There was lightness in Justin's voice. Tapping his index finger against his temple, he said, "I guess the old thinker's not as far gone as some other parts of me."

Turning back to his herbs, he asked before taking another draw on the cup, "So, what's this history about? Why are you writing it? And what's this baby got to do with it?"

Now it was Luke's turn to momentarily disappear into his thoughts. When he resurfaced, he said, "It's the history of another kingdom, of a king unlike any other."

"Humph," Justin grunted, unimpressed. "So why are *you* writing it?"

Luke considered his words before vocalizing them. "I guess you might say I'm taking a census of sorts."

"A census?"

"Yes," Luke said, growing more confident in his line of thought. "But I'm not so much looking for those who are already a part of the kingdom—I'm going about telling people the story of this baby who became King of the kingdom. I'm inviting them to stand up and be counted as one of His subjects, as citizens of His kingdom."

"Careful there, Doc! Those are dangerous words, even today. *Especially* today."

Luke was quiet, obviously thinking about Justin's words. "Let me ask you this question," Luke finally said. "So, what do you think of Claudius?"

"Claudius is our emperor!" Justin said with the snap of military readiness and utter devotion. He went into another coughing fit with his enthusiastic exclamation.

"Yes, of course he is," Luke replied in an impassive tone. "But what I mean is, what do you think of the *man* Claudius?"

"I don't understand the question," Justin countered.

"As a man, as a human being, does he demand your loyalty? Does he inspire you? Does he capture your heart?"

"Why, yes, yes, he does," Justin said with a flat, unconvincing air.

"The bribes?" Luke queried aloud.

"We don't have independent verification of those," Justin retorted.

"And the assassination of senators?"

"Well . . ."

"And his treatment of the Jews?"

"What about the Jews?" Justin snapped.

"He's forced them all out of Rome."

"So?"

"So, is he a king for all the people? For all Romans?"

"I don't understand what you are getting at."

Luke gathered himself and then asked, "Doesn't your heart long for more? More from life? More from love? More than this world, this life, this . . . empire can offer?"

Justin turned his eyes toward the window in silence.

Luke took the silence as an opening. "Justin, aren't we all made for *more*?"

The line of inquiry was finding resonance in the heart of this man who had lived his dream and was now facing a soon, and likely painful, death. His silence was deafening.

Luke continued, "What about what comes next? What can Rome do for you when you are gripped in that final fit of coughing and gasping for a last breath that just won't come to you?

"Justin, I know a King Who won't abandon you, even then, *especially* then. In fact, He has faced and conquered death itself."

Justin cast an annoyed expression at the doctor. "What is that supposed to mean? Who are you talking about?"

Luke gently replied, "Justin, you already know Him."

"I do?"

"His name is Jesus."

"The *baby*?"

"The same. Do you know what became of Him?"

"No, why would I?"

"He escaped a death plot by Herod when just an infant."

"You mean, He was still in Bethlehem when Herod ordered the slaughter?"

"He was the reason Herod ordered the slaughter! But God sent an angel to warn His father, and they escaped. They fled to Egypt and didn't return until it was safe to do so. Then they settled in the village named Nazareth."

Justin pressed his lips together and shook his head, clearly still not seeing the point.

"There in Nazareth, He grew up. At thirty years of age, Jesus began to preach, announcing that a new kingdom—the kingdom of *God*— was at hand. He invited everyone to enter that kingdom and to bow to Him as King."

"And how'd that work out?"

"Well, actually, quite well, outside of Jerusalem."

"I suppose—I mean, I *know* anyone connected to Rome wouldn't think much of that, and I'd guess the Jewish leaders didn't either."

"Right," acknowledged Luke. "In fact, they killed Him for it."

"What! How?"

"They crucified Him."

"When?"

"Almost twenty years ago."

"But here's the thing . . ." Luke paused to consider how to proceed. "Here's the thing. Justin, He didn't stay dead."

"What?" Justin asked incredulously.

"It's true. There are hundreds of witnesses. None of the authorities could prove otherwise, though they did start some rumors trying to spin things to their advantage. And Justin . . ."

"What?"

"Before He died, He told them He would rise again. He said that His death was necessary, as a substitution for ours."

"You know what, Doc? I'm sorry," the soldier said with a weary voice. "I just don't understand."

"The prophets—Jewish prophets—foretold His coming, describing it and His life and His death in detail hundreds of years before it happened. Not just one or two generalities, but dozens of specific details."

"You seem pretty sure about this."

"I told you, I am a historian. I've done the research. But you've got to add that hundreds of eyewitnesses have reported seeing Him alive after having been crucified and buried for three days, and He predicted all that would happen!"

"Okay, so where is he now?" Justin asked.

"Before the eyes of his followers, He was taken up into the heavens alive, promising to return and establish everywhere the kingdom He'd been telling everyone about."

"So, *you* are a part of this kingdom?" Justin inquired.

"Yes, I am."

There was a long pause as each man considered all that had just passed between them. The silence was broken finally by more coughs, fresh blood, and fitful gasps for air. Tortured convulsions wrenched Justin's body.

Floriana appeared again in the doorway, tears in her eyes as she leaned her weight against the doorframe. Luke asked for more hot water as he searched his bag for a fresh batch of herbs.

This round of hacking was the worst yet. It left Justin pale, weakened, watery-eyed, and fearful. Luke tried to raise him enough to get a gulp of the steeping herbs between spasms.

With the doctor's left arm under the legionnaire's broad shoulders and the cup in his right hand, the two men found themselves face to face. Eyes of terror gazed into eyes of compassion.

Without breaking their gaze, Luke begged, "Justin, wouldn't you like to know my King? Wouldn't you like a share in His life, in a life that cannot die, a life that outlives this life? Wouldn't you like to know that peace awaits you on the other side of this final battle?"

The powerful warrior was now a broken wreck—broken not only in body, but in soul. His whole life, his highest ideals, his faithful service to the empire—none of it could stand up to the enemy that was stealing his breath from him. His greatest victories were meaningless here, now, against the enemy of death.

His lips quivered, nearly too weak to form the words. "Tell me more about this King, Jesus."

"He told us He is the Son of God. That He had come to earth to save us. That His death was the means by which He would secure this salvation. He promised to defeat death forever by rising from the dead. And, well, all the facts say He did just that. He offers this salvation not only to Jews, but to all, Gentiles included. It doesn't matter who you are or what you've done; Jesus' death covers it all."

The battle-hardened soldier of Rome managed to croak out, "What's the catch?"

"No catch. Just humble yourself, confess Jesus as King and Lord and Savior. Give Him your highest allegiance. Leave off your sin and pledge the rest of your life to Him and to His kingdom. Do that and you'll find your name is written in the Book of Life, recording you as a citizen of His kingdom."

"And that works? I mean, it has worked for *you*?"

"Justin, I can't even begin to tell you! But, yes, yes, a thousand times yes!"

Floriana had settled in on her knees on the opposite side of the bed and had heard every word. She looked with longing upon her dying husband.

Justin gathered himself and said, "Do you understand what this would mean for me?"

Luke nodded. "I think I do."

"I have lived my entire life wanting nothing but to serve Rome. I have given every ounce of my strength and devotion to this kingdom and to its Caesar. I have yearly renewed the Sacramentum, the soldier's oath, swearing that Caesar is my lord, my king, my savior."

He was quiet a moment as he collected his breath.

"I would have to utterly disavow all that I've lived for."

Luke didn't answer quickly, but he never broke his eye contact with Justin. Finally, he said, "I know. Will you, even now, at the last hour of your life, bow to Jesus as your king? Will you ask Him to forgive you and accept you into His kingdom?"

Justin was quiet.

"You're going to die one way or the other; maybe tonight, maybe next week, maybe a month from now. But, Justin, you're going to die. We all are. But what then?"

Rome's soldier took in the words without argument. There was no fight left in him. Rome had given him a lifetime of labor, a cause to believe in, a champion to defend. But other than a broken body, a parcel of land, and a trifle of a pension, what did he have to show for it? Where was Rome now? Where was Lord Caesar now? Where was Claudius the Savior in his darkest hour?

With his left hand, he motioned for Floriana to go to the chest in the corner of the room. She rose and pulled it over.

"Open it," Justin demanded. As she lifted the lid, Luke beheld the trophies of Justin's service. Medals of valor, a robe of honor, faded armor.

Justin turned his eyes to Luke. "With my sweat and blood, I earned these things and the glories they represent."

"With *His* blood, Jesus bought you to be His very own, to free you from the one enemy you could not conquer—death."

Justin nodded his head. "And He rose again," he said, repeating what he'd heard Luke report earlier.

"Yes. Justin, please. Come to Jesus. He is the King of kings, and the Lord of lords. The man I travel with loves to repeat what the prophets said about Jesus long before He ever came: 'Every knee shall bow and every tongue confess that Jesus Christ is Lord.'[1] Justin, everyone—even Caesar—will bow to Jesus one day when He comes again. The prophets said that His kingdom is an everlasting kingdom. Long after Rome is gone, Jesus' kingdom will endure."

Justin did not argue, and he did not move. But his face betrayed the colossal battle being waged inside his soul.

After a few moments, Justin turned to Floriana, pointed at the chest, and ordered with an authority of a man who had commanded many, "Take it away! Take it into the street! Be gone with it!"

Floriana's eyes widened.

"Take it!" Justin commanded.

She moved quickly, dragging it from the room.

Luke studied the soldier's face, trying to discern which direction the battle would turn. But Justin needed some time to rally his strength. When Floriana had returned to her husband's side, he said to both of them, "Help me sit up."

They lifted his upper body and managed to swing his legs over the side of the bed. They steadied him as he appeared faint. Coughs erupted again, doubling him over and threatening to roll him onto the floor. They held him tight, and Luke reached again for the mixture of herbs. As the few sips he could get down had their effect, Justin slid off the side of the bed and onto his knees.

Neither Floriana nor Luke understood what Justin was doing. On his knees with his wife and doctor flanking him on either side, Justin said, "Okay, so what do I do now?"

---

1   Philippians 2:10; cf. Isaiah 45:23

Luke and Floriana exchanged a bewildered glance. "About what?" Luke asked.

"About Jesus!" Justin said as if his intentions should have been clear to them both.

"You mean, how do you surrender yourself to Jesus as your Savior and King?"

"Yes," Justin said, "of course. What else?"

"Well," Luke started, "the only way to stand up and be counted in Jesus' kingdom is to bow your knee to Him as Lord and King."

"Okay, I've got the part about the knees down. Now what do I do? In Caesar's army we swear the Sacramentum. Does Jesus have some kind of oath I have to swear?"

"Well, not exactly. I mean, there aren't any magic words or prescribed formula. Jesus looks at the heart to see whether we mean it, but we do need to confess with our mouth that Jesus is Lord."

Luke thought a moment and then said, "Justin, you've confessed thousands of times that Caesar is lord, and you as a sometimes census-taker, have listened to many thousands of the citizens of his kingdom pledge their allegiance to him. I think if you just start speaking to Jesus, the words will come to you."

With that, Justin dropped his head and opened his lips, as if he hoped something worthy would emerge. He hesitated, then launched in:

"Jesus, this is Manius Galarius Justinius, a once-proud soldier of Rome's army and a servant of her lord, savior, and king, the Emperor Caesar. I have often sworn him to be my king and his realm to be my kingdom. I know now that Jesus, Your Son, is the only true King of this world. I have heard and believe this. I believe Jesus died—that

Jesus, Your Son, is the true and only and ultimate King. I believe you, Jesus, died to pay for my wrongdoing. Please forgive me my sins. I have heard—and believe—that You have defeated death and are alive again and that You offer eternal life to those who need it and ask for it. O, Jesus, I need this eternal life, for this life I have is about to run out. I now pledge my allegiance to You above all other gods and all other lords and all other saviors. I ask that You mark me down as a citizen of Your kingdom, for the one I've served here is failing and cannot survive."

Justin paused as if uncertain how to continue. He turned to look at Luke for some direction. He met the doctor's watery eyes and tear-streamed cheeks. A quiet but firm whisper arose from his other side as Floriana said, "Me, too, Lord Jesus! Me, too!"

And the doctor added, "Amen."

At that, the once-great soldier and the doctor-turned-historian embraced as brothers. Floriana dove into the side of her husband with both arms, and Luke gathered them both up in a hug and said through tears, "Welcome to the kingdom!"

DELIVERY DAY

A SHARD OF SUNLIGHT STABBED at Shiphrah's eyes as it broke over the eastern hills. The slap of the early morning cold startled her back to attentiveness. The night hours seemed endless, but the baby had finally arrived—safely—and that is really all that mattered. Now, mother and child both lay contentedly in one another's embrace, drifting into a peaceful sleep.

Shiphrah envied them, as a fiery pain in her head reminded her that she had missed an entire night's rest. As the midwife of Bethlehem, Shiphrah often faced sleepless nights. One could not schedule these things. When it was time, it was time. And whenever the time came, it was Shiphrah's moment to be at the mother's side. It wasn't an easy way to live, but it was the most meaningful way she could imagine.

Shiphrah had delivered virtually every child in the village over the last decade, which had given her a unique bond with every family in town. She gained her skills under the tutelage of her own mother, who had been trained by her mother, who had learned from her mother before her. As long as any of them could remember, the women of their family had shepherded the children of Bethlehem into the world. She liked to think the chain went unbroken all the way back to her famous namesake, who had saved Hebrew baby boys from the clutches of Pharaoh in Moses' day.

31

A cold burst of wind pulled at her shawl, and Shiphrah tugged it tight round her neck and scurried toward home, hopeful for a few hours' sleep.

The voice began as a distant, faint call, barely perceptible at first. It grew steadily closer and louder, until it demanded her attention.

With a spasmodic jerk, Shiphrah jolted into consciousness, realizing the voice had been real and accompanied by a gentle shaking. Her daughter, Puah, bent low over her calling, "Mother! You must awaken, Mother!"

Bolting upright and blinking her eyes for focus, Shiphrah took in the familiar look on her daughter's face and knew without a word that another baby was about to arrive. The hour was at hand, again.

Still groggy from lack of sleep, Shiphrah reached for her satchel, which was a midwife's calling card—not that she needed one in Bethlehem, but it was a mark of dignity among the women in her life. Within were the familiar tools of her trade—olive oil, soft sponges from the sea, fomentations for the easing of pain, a privacy cloth, and other strips of fabric for swaddling the child.

As she started for the door, her clearing mind took inventory of the expectant mothers of the village. Stopping short, Shiphrah turned to her daughter, asking, "Who is it? The closest to her delivery day is Hannah, but she ought not to be in labor for several more weeks."

"It is a traveler, one of the pilgrims on the road for Caesar's census."

Ah, the travelers. There had been so many already. For weeks now, the homes of the village had nearly burst in the housing of them.

Bethlehem, "the house of bread," was about to run out of not only bread, but also of gracious hospitality.

Caesar and his census—all to increase his tax revenues! And now he has stranded some poor soul heavy with child in a place far distant from her home! Shiphrah caught herself, surprised at her ungraceful thoughts.

"Well, um, whose home is she in?" Shiphrah inquired as she headed again toward the door.

"Not a *home*, Mother," her daughter replied. "Malachi's stable."

Shiphrah whirled to catch her daughter's eye. "Malachi's stable! What on earth is she doing there?"

"All the homes are full up; and the inn is occupied as well. It was all that was left."

"Oh, glory! A birth in a stable!" Shiphrah said as she left the house, the slamming of the door adding an exclamation point.

The sun was high in the sky. *How long did I sleep?* Shiphrah wondered. *Not long enough,* she thought, answering her own question.

Rounding the corner, she caught sight of Malachi's residence. Without announcement, she circled back of the house and came to the stable's entrance. There, nestled down in a fresh spread of hay, lay a woman clearly in the pains of labor. Next to her was the anxious husband. He held her hand, patting it gently, praying softly, and worrying intensely.

Shiphrah made her entrance, introduced herself, and smiled as relief and thanksgiving washed over the man's face.

"So you are 'the deliverer'?" the man asked anxiously.

It was a title Shiphrah wore uncomfortably. She delighted in her calling, but to her mind, the title had always seemed an ill fit. The mothers tagged her with it somewhere through the years she'd been bringing their children into the world. But it seemed a little too lofty, too . . . sacred.

Shiphrah nodded politely and turned the questions back to the couple. In short order, she learned that they were from Nazareth and were indeed in Bethlehem for the census, for the man was of the line of David.

"You are welcome here. You are home." *Despite the smell,* Shiphrah added in her heart.

Labor had begun as they approached town. There was nowhere else to go. Malachi had shooed the animals to the side of the stable, thrown down a fresh bed of hay, and sent word for "the deliverer."

Shiphrah set to her work, first gathering details as to the date of the conception. Yes, it was the fullness of time. She sent the father for warm water. She soothed the young mother; Mary, she learned, was her name. The details of Mary's recent journey were concerning to Shiphrah. Would the physical exertion and mental stress of this young woman's travels complicate the coming hours and perhaps endanger the child's arrival? Certainly, Shiphrah had seen less rigorous challenges endanger other births. But to everyone's relief, the next few hours disappeared as they had so many times for Shiphrah and as they never had before for Mary. All were healthy; all was right. A perfect baby boy was welcomed into the world that night.

Having delivered the baby into Mary's arms, Shiphrah set about cleaning up and gathering her things. Casually, she asked, "And what shall be his name?"

"Jesus," replied the father.

"Jesus," Shiphrah echoed softly. "A wonderful name," she added as a blessing. "And Jesus, then, is your name, sir?" she inquired.

"No," came his reply, "my name is Joseph."

Odd, she thought. "Oh, then it's a family name?" she tried again.

"No," again was the reply.

"Oh," was all Shiphrah could add now.

Joseph, sensing her uneasiness, felt a need to explain.

Shiphrah listened intently, masking her curiosity by tidying the stable. A dream. An angel. "That which is conceived in her is from the Holy Spirit."[2] "You shall call his name Jesus." "He will save his people from their sins."[3]

Okay then! thought Shiphrah. Every birth was a holy event in her eyes. She was used to parents—especially first-time parents—gushing over their child. But this was a new one for her. She took in the explanation silently, finishing her work and then bidding the new parents farewell with a promise to return to check in on everyone.

When she left the stable, night had fallen. The day's events had dropped hard on her as well, coming so closely upon the sleepless night. *Home! Supper! Sleep!* Shiphrah half mumbled to herself as she strode through the cool air of the evening.

The faraway voice called her name again. It was soft enough to be nearly imperceptible. The shaking began shortly thereafter. Both grew more pronounced and unavoidable until she again bolted upright from a sound sleep. *What now!?*

---

2   Matthew 1:20
3   Matthew 1:21; Luke 1:31

The wide eyes of Puah again met hers. "Mother, something's wrong! There's shouting in the streets! Mother, I'm frightened."

Shiphrah wrestled her foggy thoughts into the candlelight and stumbled to the window. Peering through the shutters, she saw a band of shepherds skipping down the street in full-throated chorus. *Drunkards!* she denounced them inwardly. But then she noticed that they turned down the street leading to Malachi's home. *They're going to wake the baby!* She bolted out the door and broke into a run. *You can drink yourselves silly if you want, but you will not mess with my baby!*

As she neared Malachi's barn, Shiphrah stopped short. The shepherds had run straight into the barn and thrown themselves down before the child. And they were singing. Shouting in rhythm is probably more accurate. Nothing completely coherent, but it was no drinking song. They weren't drunk, but they weren't completely in control of themselves either.

Shiphrah stood silently at the door and watched with the sense that she was beholding something decidedly special, dare she say, almost . . . holy. The shepherds grew quiet in a hush of reverence before the child. She overheard their tale of innumerable angels who appeared in heaven and proclaimed, "Unto you is born this day in the city of David a Savior, who is Christ the Lord."[4]

As Shiphrah turned the words over in her mind, she recalled the father's explanation from earlier in the day: "He will save His people from their sins."[5]

Shiphrah chose not to interrupt, for the child was contented and the parents, though a bit overwhelmed, did not appear distressed. She

---

4   Luke 2:11
5   Matthew 1:21

quietly slipped away and headed home again. Lying once more upon her mat, Shiphrah found that sleep now eluded her, despite her fatigue. *Savior? Christ? The Lord? What does all this mean?* she wondered.

The child was well, as were the parents. When they returned from a trip to Jerusalem for the circumcision on the baby's eighth day, they secured lodging and chose to settle in rather than travel back up north to Nazareth with a newborn.

Shiphrah kept an eye on the little family, though from a distance. The words she had heard about the child from the father and the shepherds often came to her mind. But her family needed her, and other babies were to be birthed. Soon life took on a familiar feel again, and Shiphrah caught up on her sleep.

Several Sabbaths after the child's arrival, the new couple joined the other residents of the village in the synagogue. The day's reading was from Isaiah. When the reader came to the words "the Deliverer will come from Zion,"[6] more than a few women turned furtive glances toward Shiphrah. Nothing overly demonstrative, but Shiphrah could feel the weight of their eyes upon her. It was done out of respect, but she pulled her head covering just a bit higher and tried to duck more deeply down within it to hide herself. *They meant well,* she told herself, but Shiphrah's face flushed red nonetheless. It was, after all, the Messiah of whom Isaiah wrote, not a midwife! Shiphrah mentally changed the subject by casting her own glance to the child Mary was holding in her arms. The others around her faded to the background

---

6   Isaiah 59:20

as her thoughts were occupied with the words of his father and the shepherds concerning him.

Weeks passed into months, months into nearly a year. Life wound on in the small village. The census travelers were a forgotten memory, except for the small family that had now settled into the rhythm of Bethlehem's life.

But then the village was again upset by visitors, this time by Magi from the east. Confusion, controversy, and much conversation swirled around their presence—not so much for their strange clothing, accent, and manners, but because of their inquiries. They were on a quest, seeking a child who had been born king . . . right there, they claimed, in Bethlehem. The citizens were confused, but the men eventually found their way to the baby Jesus and his parents. Those who were within eyeshot of the event told of extravagant gifts changing hands and of the Magi performing acts of deference and homage before the child, gesticulations so profound that some likened them to worship.

In the wake of the Magi's departure, a night fell upon Bethlehem which no one in all Israel would ever forget. Soldiers from King Herod thundered into town under cover of darkness, dealing mayhem and menace in every direction. Racing methodically from home to home, they put to the sword every male child under two years of age before the families realized what was happening. They had no opportunity to flee or even attempt to hide their children. Shiphrah lost no son of her own blood, but in a sense all the sons of Bethlehem were her children. Her cries mingled with the screams of disconsolate mothers and the wails of desolated fathers. Young blood ran thick and red through streets of Bethlehem.

Then, as quickly as they had come, the soldiers were gone. *Their absence was a welcome relief, but the absence of the baby boys created a bottomless hole in the soul of the town. The sun rose the next morning, but the darkness never lifted from Bethlehem.*

For her part, Shiphrah sat stunned for days, trance-like, nearly comatose with grief. She neither ate nor spoke. Mostly she stared blankly at the walls of her tiny home. Puah urged her to eat, to rise, to speak. *But*, thought Shiphrah, *there is no balm that can heal a wound such as this.* In time her thoughts turned to the baby Jesus. *What had become of him? What of all those hope-filled words of his father, the shepherds, and the Magi?*

The inevitable call eventually arrived again: "The deliverer is needed!"

Shiphrah rose, went, attended, aided, served, helped. But *love* came hard for her now. There was something mechanical about her ministrations. Her skill was as keen as ever, but her heart had shut down. She was aware of what was happening to her but felt powerless to deliver herself from the bonds of the brewing bitterness.

With each passing year and with each new delivery, Shiphrah's heart grew harder, stony, and cold. She was professional. She was skilled. But the tenderness had abated, and the sense of calling had evaporated. A clinical sterility slipped its bony fingers around her heart and squeezed all compassion out of her interactions with the mothers. Puah noticed it before anyone else: a sharp statement; a crisp rebuke; a stinging reproof. Yes, she was being taught by her mother to birth children, but she was no longer being trained as a caregiver, for care is sometimes too heavy a burden for a wounded heart to bear.

Sometime during the next year, a caravan of travelers arrived from the south. Among them was a child with something familiar in his face. The toddler boy ran and played, stumbled and fell, laughed and cried like the little boys of Bethlehem had once done. But when one afternoon Shiphrah heard his father cry out, "Careful, Jesus!" her heart leapt. That name! That voice. That woman. *That baby!*

He's alive! Shiphrah nearly shouted it aloud in the street. She clutched her shawl over her mouth to muffle the sound. *How? I assumed . . . When did they leave? How did they know?* The questions raced through her mind faster than she could imagine answers to them.

Oh, but it doesn't really matter, does it? she told herself. One of the boys—one of *her* boys—had survived that dreadful night.

The pain did not leave entirely, but there was—at every thought of that little boy—something else mingled with it, something that seemed almost like a flicker of hope.

When the family left Bethlehem to return to their hometown of Nazareth, Shiphrah's heart sank. *But location doesn't really matter,* she consoled herself. *Jesus is alive!* Back from the dead, as it were. There was a measure of consolation in this—at least enough that she could give herself again to her calling, to the babies, and to the mothers who depended upon her.

Weeks faded into months; years turned like leaves in the wind. Decades rolled by. Shiphrah had now handed off most of the deliveries to Puah, who had apprenticed under her watchful eye.

Occasionally Shiphrah still took the call and made the delivery, but the any-time-of-the-night calls had taken their toll. Though she was no less passionate about the work, her body simply didn't allow her heart to fulfill its desires as often as it once had.

Recently Shiphrah had become more attentive to scattered reports that rode into Bethlehem with passing travelers. Someone named Jesus was making extraordinary claims, teaching unheard of things, doing things that, well, one would think only *God* could do. Healings—even returning a little boy to life!

Could this be my *Jesus?* Shiphrah wondered.

Shiphrah insisted that Puah take her to Jerusalem for the next Passover. She must see Jesus all grown up. She wished to hear him, to make up her own mind about him.

At Shiphrah's age the trudge to Jerusalem was no longer an easy trip. But the determination of her heart overrode the frailty of her body, and she found herself in the capital city, swept along among the festival crowds. She had Puah under strict orders to find out if Jesus had arrived. Quite a scene, they discovered, had played out the day before as Jesus and his disciples were welcomed into Jerusalem by singing crowds, celebrating his arrival in Messianic choruses of praise.

"To the temple!" Shiphrah commanded her daughter. Off they went, the narrow streets clogged with pilgrim feet. As they rounded a corner, the flow of humanity slowed and then ground to a halt.

"What's happening?" Shiphrah queried Puah.

"I'm not sure, Mother."

"Wait! Someone said the name Jesus." Straining to extend herself to her full height, Puah caught bits of conversation and echoed them to her stooped mother—"scribes and priests," "coins," something about taxes. "Oh Mother, I just can't hear it all!" she exclaimed in distress.

Then like a wave rolling in on the Sea of Galilee, the final sentence came: "Render to Caesar the things that are Caesar's, and to God the things that are God's."[7]

Caesar! Shiphrah's heart protested. *Caesar! What on earth rightly belongs to Caesar? Is not all God's and God's alone?* Dark memories of that murderous night long ago flamed up like dry tender to the spark. An old bitterness instantly roared back to life within her.

Shiphrah gazed with both anger and confusion into her daughter's eyes, begging for an explanation. The look frightened Puah. It reminded her of days she wished never to remember. A shrug served as her silent confession of ignorance.

The crowd slowly unknotted and began to drift onward toward the Temple. Mother and daughter were carried along in its flow. Entering the outer courtyard, Puah exclaimed, "Mother! Don't gawk, but Jesus is over along the wall. See? Over there! There's just a handful around him."

"Let's see if we can get close enough to hear more," Shiphrah suggested, and they purposely meandered in Jesus' direction. He was casually conversing with some men who seemed to be friends. Just as they were passing by, Jesus raised his hand and pointed across the way toward the offering box. He pointed out an elderly woman, not so different in appearance from Shiphrah herself.

"What's He saying?" Shiphrah demanded with a stage whisper.

"Shh! Mother! I can't hear him if you keep asking me questions!"

"He's talking about the money she put in the offering box. He said that her two coins were all she had. He is praising her."

---

7   Luke 20:25

Now Shiphrah was totally confused. First, he said that money belonged to Caesar and now he is praising a woman just like her for giving it all to God. This wasn't quite what she had expected. *He* wasn't quite what she had expected or hoped for.

"I'm tired, dear." She sighed. "Could we find our room and rest?" Shiphrah needed to think as much as she needed to rest, but it was easier to confess fatigue than confusion. Puah led her out of the Temple courts, through the streets, and to the home in which they would be staying.

The next days were again filled with efforts to see and hear Jesus. Nothing really cleared Shiphrah's mind or put it at rest. She was glad to be in attendance at Passover. There was comfort in that. But she hated the proximity to all things Roman. Soldiers were around every corner. Banners signifying Rome's heavy-handed authority hung conspicuously at every turn.

With each encounter bitterness rose like a wraith from a dark cavern in her soul. Wrapping its skeletal limbs around her heart, it was again threatening to wring all love and compassion from Shiphrah's being. Her heart wrenched in her chest, but that was nothing compared to the old chill that was blowing through her soul.

The sun had barely risen over the Mount of Olives when Puah knelt at her mother's side and whispered in her ear: "Mother! You have to wake up, Mother!"

Her first thoughts were familiar ones, experienced countless times over many years: a distressed mother drenched in a cold sweat and a baby desperately fighting through the narrows, reaching for the new world in which it must live out its existence. But as Shiphrah came to consciousness, her daughter was not calling her to attend at another birth, but to events that would usher in the opposite end of human experience.

"Mother! Something is happening. Jesus was arrested in the night."

A youthful surge of energy shot through Shiphrah's body, and she sprang upright. Wrapping her shawl around her, she followed Puah out the door and down the street. As they neared Pilate's quarters, the gathered crowd had swelled and the energy in it felt more mob-like than that of pilgrims gathering for worship. Clearly the women from Bethlehem were arriving in the midst of events that had been unfolding for hours. There was no time to catch up on the details.

Pilate appeared and lifted his voice: "I am bringing him out to you that you may know that I find no guilt in him."[8]

Two soldiers manhandled Jesus into the light. He stood before the crowd bloodied and barely upright. His nearly naked body was draped in a purple robe and his head was crowned with thorns.

Pilate again raised his voice: "Behold the man!"[9]

What madness is this? What are they doing? What has he done?

Shiphrah's silent query was interrupted by the chorus of the crowd: "If you release this man, you are not Caesar's friend. Everyone who makes himself a king opposes Caesar."[10]

It was all too much and coming at her too fast. *What in God's name is happening here? Has Jesus claimed to be the Jew's king? And why would this crowd now care about friendship with Caesar?*

Then the crowd's voice was raised as one to the Roman governor. They shouted over and over again, "Crucify him!" and "We have no king but Caesar!"[11]

---

8   Luke 23:4
9   John 19:5
10 John 19:12
11 John 19:15

Shiphrah crumpled to the ground. Her legs could no longer bear the weight of a lifetime spent attending to the Jewish race at its most vulnerable moment, in bitter hatred toward Rome for its disregard for Jewish life. To hear the Jews themselves crying out loyalty to Rome's king and demanding the death of one of their own, one of *her* own . . . it was simply more than she could bear.

"Mother!" cried Puah.

Bending low, Puah tried to right her, but all she could do was wrap her mother in her arms to shield her from the wild press of legs and feet all about her.

As the crowd finally began to disperse, Puah laid her mother's head gently back and asked, "Mother, are you all right? Mother! Say something!"

"We must go to him," was all Shiphrah could muster.

"Who, mother?"

"Jesus."

"Mother, no. You aren't strong enough. I don't even know where they've taken him."

"Where do you think they've taken him, my love?" Shiphrah asked.

Yes, Puah knew, of course. But to say it was more than even she could bear.

"Mother, no," she protested again.

"Yes, dear. We must. If it is the last thing I do, I must go to him."

Puah retrieved some water. Shiphrah sipped. Puah bathed her brow. Up she came, with Puah's gentle assistance, and they were off, through the streets, headed for the Place of a Skull.

By the time they crested the hill, the soldiers had already suspended Jesus high upon the cross. Nausea washed over both mother and daughter as they took in the sight. They had given themselves to bringing life into the world. They had no stomach for seeing it snuffed out.

They drew as near as they dared. Others stood about as well. Soldiers. Mockers. There were others, also, who were clearly moved to deep sorrow by the scene playing out before them. But like the midwives, they, too, were unable to tear themselves away from the horror on the hill.

Then came His voice—raspy and hoarse, yet clear and strong. With His crucifiers gambling for His clothing at His blood-stained feet, Jesus prayed, "Father, forgive them, for they know not what they do."[12]

Shiphrah nearly sank again, this time not under the weight of her burden, but under the authority of Jesus' words.

Forgive them? Forgive them?! She grew lightheaded and felt a swoon washing over her, but she remained upright. Images came rushing back from the past, long buried and locked away in the cavernous chamber that had been dug out of her heart that night so long ago. *That night! Soldiers. Swords. Blood! Cries! Tiny bodies draped in the arms of wailing parents; a scarlet syrup dripping from little limbs.*

It was too much; her knees gave way. If Puah had not already had her hands on her mother's arms, Shiphrah would have taken a frightful fall. Instead, she slunk to the ground again, guided by Puah's able arms.

The others barely noticed, transfixed by the scene before them. Puah cradled her mother, hoping and praying that her life would not also end on this fateful day.

Sparkling stars seemed to dance against the darkness at the back of Shiphrah's eyelids. Her daughter's voice called to her as if from a

---

12 Luke 23:34

distant land, begging her to come to her again. When her eyes opened, the darkness of her eyelids was matched by the darkness that had descended over the land.

Fighting to bring her thoughts to clarity, Shiphrah heard someone in the crowd half-whispering familiar words. She recognized them from the synagogue, words of the prophet Isaiah . . .

"He was despised and rejected by men . . ."[13]

"Surely he has borne our griefs and carried our sorrows . . ."[14]

" . . . upon him was the chastisement that brought us peace."[15]

" . . . he bore the sin of many, and makes intercession for the transgressors."[16]

Shiphrah stirred, and with Puah's assistance rose again to her feet.

She raised her eyes to look upon Jesus and take in the full panorama of the events before her. By some strange power that had entered her soul, it seemed as if she could see not only the physical realities before her, but the breadth of time and eternity, of heaven and earth melded together in this singular moment. Shiphrah was overcome with an awareness that what was happening here would prove to be the pivot point of not only her life, but of life itself.

Jesus' voice interrupted her thoughts one more time. The hoarseness remained, but the tone was stronger, clearer, almost triumphant. More like a trumpet blast than a human voice, it was not the cry of a martyr, but of a victor. It was not a cry of surrender, but of command—directing, announcing, declaring: "It is finished!"[17]

And with that, his head slumped down upon his chest. He was gone.

---

13   Isaiah 53:3
14   Isaiah 53:4
15   Isaiah 53:5
16   Isaiah 53:12
17   John 19:30

Shiphrah gazed upon Jesus' body, limp upon the cross. "My Jesus," she said softly under her breath. "Now they are gone, *all* of them, all my boys of Bethlehem."

The crowd began to filter away, with Shiphrah and Puah among them. A few of the other onlookers, after studying the two women for a while, asked if they wanted to join them for a time of prayer. Shiphrah and Puah accepted their invitation, feeling mysteriously drawn to do so. And though these followers of Jesus were previously strangers to the two midwives, it didn't take long to feel as if they'd shared a lifetime with one another. Something unseen but powerful bound their hearts as one.

Two days later, Passover was complete. The sun rose on Sunday, and Shiphrah and Puah were intent on making the return trek to Bethlehem. But suddenly, the door flew open, and one of their new friends appeared: "He's gone!"

"Who?" Puah asked.

"Jesus!"

"Gone? Gone where?"

"From the grave. The stone has been rolled away. His body isn't there! You've got to come pray with us."

As they entered the room where they'd gathered after the events of Golgotha, they could sense a change in the atmosphere. There was a hope that had been absent before. Some of the women were telling their story—of actually meeting Jesus. "He really is," they said, "alive!"

Two of the men insisted that the tomb had been empty when they'd arrived there earlier in morning.

Could it be? How *could it be?* Shiphrah wondered.

Then, late in the day, two other disciples told the story of Jesus appearing to them as they walked along the road toward their home.

Neither Shiphrah nor her daughter could discount the multiplying witnesses, but they couldn't explain them either. Nor could they quite believe them. Yet they didn't quite *dis*believe them.

As they were caught up in the conversations, questions, and doubts, He somehow slipped into the room unannounced. They felt His presence before they saw His body. *Jesus!* Their stunned silence soon morphed into a holy hush.

Shiphrah and Puah, like the rest, found themselves prostrate before him, overcome and overwrought by his presence.

Shiphrah heard the voice before she realized it was her own. It was but a whisper, but as crystal clear to her as any thought she'd ever had: "My Jesus; my . . . hope."

Jesus spoke, briefly, and then departed as mysteriously and effortlessly as he'd come. For Shiphrah, even more memorable than the words he had spoken was the look he had cast into her eyes. He did not so much look *at* her, as *through* her . . . into places she'd not wanted to admit existed in her heart. And with that look, Jesus' presence filled, possessed, and transformed all those dark places. Her entire heart softened, became pliable; it beat again with life—life of a flavor she'd never tasted before, of a hue she'd never seen, of a song that had never fallen upon her ear.

Her heart cried out in an exchange that passed as clearly between her and Jesus as if it had been sealed before the elders in the gates of Bethlehem. She signed on to the new covenant with her own simple, inward confession: "Jesus, my King. Jesus, my God!"

Then just like that He was gone—from the room, but not from her heart. But something else *was* gone from her heart. It had been vanquished when Jesus moved in. Darkness had fled at the light of his presence. Bitterness had broken like a dam before the flood of his love. Sharp splinters of hate had been swept away by the wind of the Spirit blowing through her.

Mother and daughter gazed into one another's eyes in a way that only two people who have shared a life-changing, eternity-transforming experience can know. All Shiphrah could think of were the words from Isaiah that had felt uncomfortable when applied to her, but were now filled with a wonderful new meaning about her Savior: "The Deliverer will come . . . he will banish ungodliness . . . and this will be my covenant with them when I take away their sins."[18]

Puah broke the silence: "Mother, I'm free!"

To which Shiphrah replied, "I know. Me too. I feel like a newborn baby."

18 Isaiah 59:20

Easter

THE LOST SHEPHERD

THE NIGHT AIR CARRIED A chill and slipped it down the back of Eli's tunic. A shiver ran down his spine. Instinctively, he pulled his cloak a little tighter around his neck. The blue-black sky was salted with the light of many thousands of stars. A thumbnail moon hung on the far horizon like a tipped bowl ready to spill its contents.

It was another night shift in the fields outside Bethlehem. A hundred sheep were bedded down in the grasses sprawling out below him. The night stretched on in a way that those who do their business during the day can never quite imagine.

Other flocks rested not far away, and Eli knew their shepherds were also nestled somewhere along the hillside, watching over their flocks by night. He caught the sound of padding feet approaching from behind him and to the right and turned to see Amos making his way toward him. The two men greeted one another, and Amos took a spot next to Eli. Quietness enveloped them for a few moments; theirs was the comfortable familiarity of a relationship forged over long years together on these solitary hills.

Finally, Amos spoke. "Carmi and I made the third-watch rounds. Bad news."

"What now?" asked a weary Eli.

"The count came out at only ninety-nine."

"Whose flock?" Eli asked, already knowing the answer.

"Yours."

51

"Okay." Eli sighed. And with that, he rose and disappeared down the hill.

Amos softly called after him, "I'll keep an eye on your flocks till you get back."

Eli never turned but raised his hand to acknowledge Amos' promise, as if to say, "Thanks, my friend!"

The search took longer than Eli expected. The valley gave up no lost sheep, so he had to cross over the ridge and search behind the next spine of hills. Finally, he'd found the lost one mindlessly wandering alone on a dark and deserted stretch of open pasture.

He lovingly scolded the wanderer as he approached. At the sound of Eli's voice, the ewe snapped her head in his direction. In the dim light, he thought he could make out an expression of familiarity and relief in the sheep's eyes. Dropping to his knees, he ducked his head under her belly and pinned her front legs together in his right hand and her back legs in his left. With a little more effort than he expected to use, he stood upright, the still-chewing lamb resting across his shoulders.

Eli's lungs burned with heavy breaths, and his lower back squawked with a dull ache as he rejoined his flock. He dropped once again to his knees and gently placed the lost sheep on the dewy grass among the others of his flock. As he rose, he ran his hand firmly but lovingly across the back of her neck as if to say, "Welcome home. Now, stay put!"

He turned and made his way back up the hill from which he could once again watch over the flock committed to his charge. But he didn't find Amos where he had left him.

Hmmm, he thought, *he must have split the difference between his flock and mine.* So he wandered to the left for a while, just to let Amos know he was back. But he found no Amos. *That's odd,* he thought. *I've never known Amos to leave the flock unattended . . . for any reason.*

Eli decided to sit right there, equidistant from his flock and Amos'. He could see them all from here, anyway. They'd figure this out when the sun came up.

As the eastern ridge was just beginning to grow rosy, Eli saw something that made him rub his eyes and look again. Actually, he wasn't sure if he first saw them or *heard* them. They were all there—Amos, Shlomo, Carmi, and Uri—the whole night crew that had frequented these hills for years. But they were *together*—not each one with his flock. And they were running, jumping, hooting, hollering, shouting, singing—he couldn't quite tell which best described their approach.

Sheep began to rustle uncomfortably. Eli welcomed the merry band with a wrinkled forehead and a mouth hanging open in disbelief. He was speechless. They were not. In fact, they all talked at once—falling over one another in their excitement to tell Eli a story that strained credulity.

Angels! Light! Glory! Bethlehem! King! Baby! Manger!

The words tumbled out in an incoherent jumble.

Before long, the sun had broken over the far line of hills, and the day crew arrived. They, too, were subjected to the tales of wonder. They, too, scratched their heads in confusion.

As they made their way toward their homes, the four walked together. Eli trailed behind, watching, wondering. He didn't understand. But it was clear that whatever the others experienced in his absence had bound them together in a new brotherhood. It created a fellowship that he didn't understand, one that connected them in the bonds of common experience even more than all their years together in the fields. Just like that—while doing his duty by faithfully seeking a lost sheep—Eli had become an outsider. Not that the others didn't try to include him, but he had simply missed out on this heavenly encounter, on this introduction to the Child-king of whom they spoke.

Months unfolded into a year, and years piled one upon another, stretching into decades. Lambs lived and died—many of them as sacrifices of worship at the temple in Jerusalem. But the flock remained constant; always, there was a flock to tend. The same five men worked the same hills together into their older years. But nothing in those years of common existence and labor admitted Eli into the fellowship created on that miraculous night so long ago. It wasn't that Amos, Shlomo, Carmi, and Uri purposefully excluded Eli. In fact, they spoke often to him of that night. But he hadn't been there. It was *their* experience, not his.

As festival time drew near once again, Eli and his friends selected the choicest of their herds. They made the plodding journey toward Jerusalem, their lambs destined to end their days as expressions of someone's plea for forgiveness, offered up on the altar to God.

Soon after their arrival, they set up shop, and pilgrims who had also recently arrived began haggling with them. The streets were busy and noisy—a cacophony of voices, animals bleating, and cart wheels. It was all a bit dizzying for Eli, who was more accustomed to the quiet, lonely nights on the hills near Bethlehem. Dutifully, he sat, keeping a careful eye upon his lambs. Watching was, after all, what shepherds do best. And people-watching does have its own kind of entertainment value. *Where do all these people come from?* Eli wondered to himself. It felt like all of Abraham's children had descended upon this one little corner of Jerusalem.

Then his eyes landed upon a solitary figure standing across the way, back against the wall. He, too, was watching. But there was something different about Him, something in his eyes. Something in the way He watched the people, almost as if He was watching *over* the people. Was it concern? Or maybe pity? Love, perhaps? Eli couldn't quite tell. Certainly, there was a tinge of sadness in the stranger's countenance.

Eli made himself look away, not wanting to gawk like some bumpkin who'd never been to the big city before. But almost involuntarily, his eyes were drawn back—again and again. And every time he saw Him, he saw Him seeing people. There was something strangely familiar about it—almost shepherd-like, as if He were watching over the people like Eli did with his flock. Though He looked upon them all, it somehow seemed that He saw them each one—harassed and helpless, as if they were lost sheep without a shepherd.

Then once, as his eyes drifted back toward the Stranger, Eli nearly jumped out of his skin, for the Stranger was looking back at him. And not just *at* him, but *into* his eyes—almost, it seemed, into his heart!

Eli forced his gaze away as quickly as possible, toward some innocuous spot on a wall. He tried to look nonchalant, but those eyes had seized him. It felt as if he were still in their grip, even though he had averted his eyes.

Suddenly, Eli's trance was broken by the loud voice next to him. "How much for this one?" asked an insistent man with a perturbed look on his face. *How many times has he asked that and I didn't hear him?* Eli wondered, a bit embarrassed.

Eli closed the sale and was preoccupied for several more hours by the pressing crowds and their inquiries about his lambs. But that night, when he laid his head down to sleep, his mind filled with the image of that Stranger's face and that look in His eyes.

A couple of days later, after all the men's sheep had been sold, Eli and Amos walked the streets of the city before beginning their journey home to flocks and families. The country boys walked, mostly without talking, simply absorbing the sights, sounds, and smells of the pressing festival crowds. Then Eli saw him across the way at the corner of two streets. The man from the market. But he wasn't alone now. And he wasn't watching; he was speaking to a gathering crowd. Eli grabbed a handful of Amos's tunic sleeve and pulled him, without a word, to the edge of the listeners.

If this man's countenance had been captivating, his words were magical. Those gathered immersed themselves silently in his teaching. These were the first words Eli and Amos heard him say: "What man of you, having a hundred sheep, if he has lost one of them, does not leave the ninety-nine in the open country, and go after the one that is lost, until he finds it? And when he has found it, he lays it on his shoulders, rejoicing."[19]

Eli was stunned, lost in his thoughts. It wasn't exactly a trade secret, but there was something about the way the stranger said the words and the stirring they created in Eli's heart. It was as if the man had locked eyes with Eli and said, "I understand" in a way that left no doubt in Eli's heart that indeed he did.

The current of the pushing crowds carried Eli and Amos partially down the street, against their wishes.

---

19 Luke 15:4

In the confusion, Eli asked Amos, "Who is that man?"

Amos shrugged and said, "Some Rabbi they call Jesus."

Eli descended again into his thoughts. What was it about this Man that so captivated him?

Just then, Shlomo, Carmi, and Uri called out from across the way. Soon, they were all together and heading down the path toward home.

A year later, another festival season rolled around, and the five shepherds found themselves again in Jerusalem with that year's best-of-the-flock. Once again, the sheep were sold, one haggling transaction at a time. Once again, the five shepherds walked the streets of the capital city before heading home.

Eli conjectured, almost hoped. *Any chance the same Rabbi might show up again at the festival?* In the dark of many long nights, Eli had wondered about the Rabbi, the magnetic nature of His countenance, and the riveting words he had spoken. Eli even inquired—quietly, so that the others didn't know—if anyone had heard if the Rabbi Jesus was in town. When a passerby said they thought He might be in the temple courts, Eli gently steered the little huddle of shepherds in that direction.

There he is! Eli realized. He pushed through the crowds, temporarily separating himself from the other four. It was hard to hold his place in the push and shove of the masses, but he made out one sentence. "The Son of Man came to seek and to save the lost!"[20]

What? What's lost? Who's lost? Lost from what? But the tides of humanity pushed him out of earshot, and he didn't hear where the rest of the sermon went.

---

20 Luke 19:10

Eli knew that before they left for home he had to hear more from the Teacher. The others finally caught up with him, shouting, "Hey, where'd you go? Thought we'd lost you!"

After supper, the crowds began to thin, and the streets weren't so full. The temple was still filled, but it was a quieter place now. Eli nodded to the other four in the direction of the far corner where the crowd had gathered. They quietly took their place on the fringe of the assembly and listened in on the sermon.

Jesus was saying, "Truly, truly, I say to you . . . he who enters by the door is the shepherd of the sheep . . . the sheep hear his voice, and he calls his own sheep by name and leads them out. When he has brought out all his own, he goes before them, and the sheep follow him, for they know his voice. A stranger they will not follow, but they will flee from him, for they do not know the voice of strangers. . . . I am the good shepherd. The good shepherd lays down his life for the sheep . . . I am the good shepherd. I know my own and my own know me, just as the Father knows me and I know the Father; and I lay down my life for the sheep. And I have other sheep that are not of this fold. I must bring them also, and they will listen to my voice. . . . My sheep hear my voice, and I know them, and they follow me."[21]

Lost in his thoughts, Eli felt a tug on the back of his collar. It was Shlomo, wearing an expression that said, "Come on! Let's go."

As their feet stirred the dust on the road to home, Eli emerged from his thoughts and asked the others, "What do you think He means?"

The four turned their heads, surprised to hear something from the dreamer. "What did *who* mean?"

"Jesus," Eli replied.

---

21   John 10:1-15

"Mean about what?"

"Well, like when he said, 'I am the good shepherd.'"

Silence answered his inquiry.

But he continued, "Or when He said, 'My sheep heard my voice, and I know them, and they follow me'?"[22]

"Uh, well, we're not exactly theological types, are we?" Carmi offered.

But Eli wouldn't be dissuaded. "He said, 'He calls his own sheep by name and leads them out.' I don't get it! But I can't stop thinking about it either."

Eight eyes rolled; four mouths shut. The quintet walked on in thoughtful silence.

A couple of weeks later, the five of them were sitting around a common fire to ward off the night chill. Amos, for the umpteenth time, raised the topic of that glorious night that transpired on these hills decades before.

"Guys, remember the color of that angel?" he queried.

"It wasn't the one angel that rocked me," said Shlomo. "It was the multitude of the heavenly host that 'bout scared me out of my sandals!"

"It was the sight of the Baby in the manger that sealed it for me," Carmi added. And with that, the saga unfolded, as it had so often over the years.

The band of four reveled in the mystery of their common encounter. Though still at the fire, Eli felt utterly alone.

"Whatever came of Him?" Eli asked.

Silence fell over the four. Eli never spoke during their recollections.

"Um, what?" Amos said.

---

22 John 10:1-15

"What do you suppose ever came of Him?" Eli repeated.

"Of Whom?" Carmi asked.

"Of the Baby."

"Well," said Uri with raised eyebrows, "I—I don't know." With that, glances were passed around the fire, and silence added the punctuation.

Eli broke the awkward silence: "Do you think we could find out?"

"Well," offered Uri again, "I did hear that his family had fled to Egypt. But after that, who knows."

Persistent, Eli asked, "What was His name?"

"The Baby's?"

"Yes, the Baby's! What was His name?"

"I don't know. They probably didn't name Him till eight days later when they offered their sacrifices at the temple," said Carmi.

"But remember what the angel did say," offered Amos.

"What?"

"That when we found the Baby, we would have found the Christ, the very Lord Himself."

"Yes, well," Uri inserted, like a period intended to end the discussion. They'd speculated about all this before, but it had gotten them nowhere.

Eli wouldn't let it rest, however: "Do you think the innkeeper would know?"

"He's been dead for ten years! And when the Baby's family left town, they didn't want to be found."

"But we could ask the innkeeper's family if they know anything."

"Why are you suddenly so interested in all this?" Amos inquired. "You've never offered so much as a peep over all these years when we start reminiscing about that night."

"That's because it is *your* story, not mine," Eli said, with deep emotion fueling his pronunciation of the word "your." It felt good to say it, almost as if a long-festering boil had been lanced.

"That night divided us," he said. "Ever since, it has been you four . . . and then me."

"What are you talking about?" Shlomo protested. "Of course, you're one of us! How many nights have we sat here together watching over our flocks?"

"True, but in the most defining night of your lives, I was on the other side of those hills," Eli said as he raised his right hand and pointed toward the shadowy blue hills. "I was lost in the dark, out seeking a stray when God visited you."

The shepherds retreated into the familiar comfort of silence. No reply could change the realities that night had foisted upon their little band. The divide of the Divine had been real, though unintended, and unspoken until now.

As if they'd all silently contracted to avoid any serious conversation, the following days were filled mostly with small talk. Then one evening, as the embers in the fire burned low, and faces were hard to distinguish in its ebbing glow, Uri broke the contract.

"Hey, guys," he said in a tone that betrayed the fact that he was about to venture into uncomfortable territory.

"Well," Uri continued hesitantly, "I dropped by the inn the other day."

Somehow, he knew every head had turned his way, and though they couldn't see his face, nor he theirs, they were all looking directly at his shadowy silhouette. Their collective silence begged Uri to keep carrying the weight of this conversation. "So, thing is, the family didn't really know much, but they did say they thought the father's name was Joseph. And they had a fragment of a memory that he may have been a carpenter."

There! Uri thought. *I've broken the moratorium on the topic, and now it is someone else's turn to run with this.*

Carmi admitted that it rang a bell, now that Uri mentioned it.

Amos somewhat reluctantly carried the second part of the conversation. "I've been asking around, too," he confessed. "Someone in town thought the family had later returned from Egypt, settling in Nazareth."

"Nazareth!" Shlomo exclaimed. But the fact was he'd been doing a little investigation of his own. This whole "Christ, the Lord" memory had left him unsettled. After a pause, he admitted, "I went to a local teacher and asked a few questions."

"Like what?" Eli asked.

"I wanted to know if the prophets in any way connect the hope of Messiah with Bethlehem."

"Oh, come on!" Eli objected, as if almost incensed by the idea.

"At least let him finish!" insisted Uri.

Shlomo continued, "The teacher said he'd have to get back to me. And a few days later, he did. He said the prophet Micah wrote, 'And you, O Bethlehem, in the land of Judah, are by no means least among the rulers of Judah; for from you shall come a ruler . . .'"[23] He paused for effect. "Are you guys ready for this?"

"For what?" they all cried in exasperation.

Shlomo continued, "'From you shall come a ruler who will *shepherd* my people Israel.'"

---

23 Micah 5:2

The Messiah a Shepherd? Eli rolled the unlikely thought through his mind.

By their collective silence, the others admitted their skepticism as well. *As shepherds, we're necessary but unwelcome members of society. By most, considered uncouth, unaccepted, and largely unwanted. The Messiah a Shepherd?*

Try as he might, Eli just couldn't get his head around the idea.

They'd always wondered why they were chosen to share such a remarkable welcome for the new Child. This added a new dimension to their speculation. *Who more appropriate to welcome the Messiah than shepherds, if that's what the prophecy said.*

"That's not all," Uri interjected.

"What now?" Carmi sighed, as if at the end of his patience.

"They believe His given name may be Jesus."

Whoa! Nobody said it, but everybody thought it. Or *felt* it.

This was too much, over the top, for a bunch of reserved shepherds. The long hours of that night slipped by quickly as each mind was awhirl, trying to make sense of these things.

Several months later, they were on their way to Jerusalem again for Passover. But they all knew that this time, they were not merely there to sell lambs; they were there hoping to see Jesus again.

The city was as crowded, maybe more so than in past visits. But there was something in the air other than the electricity of large crowds. It was hard to put a finger on it. Even during the routine arguments about prices with customers, there was confusion, maybe, or fear—something ominous. Something indefinable, but undeniable.

They inquired about Jesus when they could, trying not to look too obvious. But the reports were mixed—praise on one hand, poison on the other. The tides of public opinion about Jesus were changing, and not for the better.

Late Thursday afternoon, the last of their lambs were sold. The shepherds were free now to move around the city, seeking to find Jesus. People had seen Him that week—that much was clear. But no one could tell them where He might be.

The next morning, they searched again but were met with suspicious expressions and evasive answers. Something was up, but they didn't know exactly what it was. Then they heard a commotion at the end of the street. People shouted; women screamed; and children ran to get a look at something and then fled in tears.

Eli, Amos, Shlomo, Carmi, and Uri raced to the end of the street and pressed through the crowds. They arrived just in time to see a gruesome parade disappearing around the next corner—all appearing to be centered around a bloodied, beaten Form slumped under a heavy, wooden cross.

Then they heard it—all at the same moment—the name, "Jesus!"

What? That was Jesus? How? Why? The questions tumbled through their minds.

Their feet began to move in unison. As if in some previously agreed-upon plan, they headed off in the direction of the parade.

They didn't catch up with the crowd until they were outside the city. There, they followed at a distance up the hill called Golgotha. In stunned silence, they watched as the brutalized, bloody Rabbi was nailed by His hands and feet to the beams and the whole cross was dropped with a stomach-wrenching thud into a hole hewn in the solid rock.

There they stood, mouths agape. Silent. Uncomprehending, but unwilling to flee. Hours flowed by as they kept their silent, stupefied vigil.

The skies grew dark; blackness settled over them, over the entire land. Darkness was something they knew well—they worked the night shift, after all. But this was more than the absence of light; there was something fuller, heavier about this. There was something almost spiritual about it.

The crowds thinned. They'd gotten their fill of gore and moved on to other attractions. No one counted how many remained or sized them up to figure out why they might have stayed. All were transfixed by the Figure on the center cross.

Neither Eli nor the others had really noticed just how huddled they'd become with a handful of others who were there. Strangers, but somehow not, welded in a fellowship they had not desired or pursued. Eli became cognizant of this, however, when one of them—a young man standing nearly shoulder to shoulder with him—seemed to say, almost subconsciously and under his breath, "All we like sheep have gone astray; we have turned—every one—to his own way; and the Lord has laid on him the iniquity of us all."[24]

"What's that?" Eli found himself saying, turning his head momentarily to see who had spoken.

"Isaiah," the man mumbled without moving his fixed gaze from the form before him.

Each retreated again into their silence.

---

24   Isaiah 53:6

But then it was Eli's turn to mutter, "The good shepherd lays down his life for the sheep."[25]

There's no way Jesus could have heard him. The man next to him hadn't even seemed to notice. But at that precise moment, Jesus lifted His head. Through stringy locks of hair matted with drying blood and with bruised and swollen eyes, his gaze met Eli's.

These were the same eyes that had fixed on Him in the market. And there it was again—that *something* in His eyes. A penetrating, soul-boring, heart-piercing something. It was so powerful that Eli was surprised it didn't hurt. But the sensation felt more like love!

And suddenly, Eli realized—right there, eye-to-eye with Jesus in the last moments of His life—*Somehow He heard me! And somehow He knows.*

Though there was the sound of approaching death in Jesus' breathing, there was love in His eyes. And they held Eli in their gaze for an eternal moment of redemptive compassion.

Then Jesus' head bowed again, as His agonies spiked.

But Eli would never escape that gaze. His thoughts ran wild within him: *He knows! He knows me! He knows that I know. He was there, that night—not just in a manger, but on the far side of the ridge. While the angels announced His birth to my friends, He was also where I was on the other side of the hill, the "wrong" side of the hill . . . looking, seeking . . .*

The thoughts in Eli's head became words in his mouth; and Amos, Carmi, Uri, and Shlomo heard the soft question rise from his lips, "'What man of you, having a hundred sheep, if he has lost one of them, does not leave the ninety-nine in the open country, and go after the one that is lost, until he finds it? And when he has found it, he lays it on his shoulders, rejoicing.'"[26]

"What's that?" Amos muttered.

"He knows!" was all Eli could whisper.

Then the man next to him said, "'Like a sheep he was led to the slaughter and like a lamb before its shearer is silent, so he opens not his mouth.'"[27]

And so the scene played out. Each one stayed on, all five of them, watching to the bitter end.

After Jesus' body was taken down from the cross, they silently put one foot in front of the other and headed toward Bethlehem. Time seemed to stand still—or perhaps it rushed on. None could tell, for they were lost in the emotions and questions provoked by what they'd experienced.

A few nights later, each one had taken his place on the hillside, his flock nestled into the grass below him. Suddenly, Carmi broke upon the scene—running, jumping, screaming something that was mostly indecipherable. It was reminiscent of the way all four had rushed to Eli that night over thirty years before.

Between gasps for air, Carmi's words tumbled out in fragments of sentences. But soon enough, they got the point. "Reports coming out of Jerusalem are saying Jesus is alive!"

But how could that be?

"His tomb is empty. His followers demand that He is alive, that they've actually seen Him. Predictably," he added, "the authorities are livid and desperate to silence this as a false report."

---

26   Luke 15:4
27   Isaiah 53:7

Night or not, flocks or not, provisioned or not, the five lit out, racing back to Jerusalem to investigate for themselves.

Upon arrival and with a little work, they were able to locate the fledgling company of Jesus-followers. They listened carefully to the firsthand accounts. It was all so hard to comprehend, but it was obvious these people had encountered something or someone out of this world.

Caught up in the fellowship and in hearing the stories again and again, the days flowed one into another. Belief in the Resurrection was gaining momentum. More and more people were joining their company; some were merely curious, others soundly convinced.

And then one day, as some five hundred of them were all together in prayer, He came among them. Jesus stood in their midst! Glorious, shining, regal! Every mouth stopped. Every eye was upon Him—drinking in the glory of His splendor.

And then, it seemed to Eli, Jesus turned and again fixed him with His eyes. These were the same eyes that had locked on him first in the market and then later from the cross, but they were somehow different now. The love in them was the same, but the authority had been multiplied.

Although no words were exchanged—and Eli never knew how long that eye-exchange between the two actually lasted—Jesus' gaze changed Eli forever. Never—not through a thousand eternities—could he escape that loving look from the Lord. Nor would he ever want to.

And then a fragment of a memory, a single sentence hidden in the back of Eli's mind, was drawn into conscious thought by some force he could neither locate nor resist: "I know my own and my own know me."[28]

---

28 John 10:14

A reverent, worshipping smile spread over Eli's face, and he uttered, "He knows!"

And in the same instant, he realized that he, himself, knew. He knew things he'd never understood before—knew them in a way that was more than information, but in a way in which the knowledge became transformative.

Eli now understood that he himself, the lowly shepherd, had all along really been a sheep—a lost lamb. He knew that he had gone his own way, but the Savior—this Jesus—was *the* Shepherd, the Good Shepherd. And Eli had now been found by Him. He also realized that he was no longer on the outside looking in. All five men—Amos, Carmi, Shlomo, Uri, and Eli—like the other 495 souls around them, were entranced by the triumphant, shining Savior-Shepherd standing in their midst.

Though Jesus would have to depart physically, they all instinctively knew that He would never leave them. They would never again be lost and alone, or on the outside looking in.

My Father's Eyes

If you could see
yourself the way
Jesus sees you...

THE WEIGHT OF WAITING

LONG, GRAY WISPS OF HAIR extended from between his clinched fingers as his balled-up hands pressed hard against his forehead. Upon his knees his body rocked in rhythmic motion as his heart wrestled with God. His eyes, shut tight in earnest pursuit of an unseen God, squeezed salty droplets from their corners that were lost in his long, white beard.

"How long, O Lord! How long!"

The lean silhouette of masculine agedness had been earned through long bouts of fasting. The sinewy strength of his soul was the product of extended seasons of earnest prayer.

"Lord, please! How long? When will I see Him? You promised me. It was your own word! You—I need not remind You—cannot lie."

His rocking slowed as he fell into outward silence. But the inward pleading continued until his kneeling form came to a frozen, statuesque stillness.

"Lord! O Lord . . . *when?*"

This had been Simeon's life ever since in a flash of inward, personal revelation, God had assured him that he would not leave this earth without seeing the Messiah.

Messiah. The Anointed One. The King. The Commander. The Conqueror. The Liberator. The Christ.

He, Simeon, would live to see Him! To witness His breaking forth upon the stage of history!

But—and how many times had he asked it by now?—*when!*

Well-advanced in age and with no peers left around him, Simeon had repeated the question "How long?" more times that he could imagine and had uttered the word "when" more than he cared to calculate. The weight of the waiting was, well, killing him. Except that he could not die until the waiting was over, which only made the sense of dying lay heavier upon his soul.

Outside of town, a young couple peeled off the road from Bethlehem and turned toward Jerusalem. As they walked, they bore a weight, a happy weight—a Child in their arms. Their Child was no burden, but the weight of all that swirled around Him did still weigh heavily upon them. He was just shy of six weeks old. Forty days ago, the burden of their anticipation had slid off their hearts as they welcomed their Son into the world. But there had been no time for boredom since then, between angel visitations and an impromptu worship service with shepherds. And, no, the leering eyes of the self-righteous still hadn't entirely lifted from them. But at least He was here now. His presence somehow lightened the load that had been bearing down upon their souls all these long months.

Emerging from one of Jerusalem's narrow, cobblestone streets, the couple with child in arms began climbing toward the massive, looming edifice of the temple. The man, Joseph, paused at the sight of one of the vendors, who had set up shop along this route to the place of worship. With a grimace, he fished a few small coins from his bag. They'd come to him the hard way—with hammer blows and sawdust. As a carpenter, he eked out a living for himself and his tiny family. There would be no lamb for his bride's ceremonial cleansing. The Law's provision of a poor man's offering would have to do.

"Two of the turtledoves, please," he asked the seller, with a hint of embarrassment in his tone. He couldn't bring himself to look his wife, Mary, in the eye during the transaction.

Though no noise entered his room and nothing changed about him, Simeon was suddenly roused from the depths of his concentrated prayer. Abruptly, he rose, grabbed his outer tunic, and exited to make his way onto the street. His prior stillness was now displaced by his present rush. With long, loping strides he ran through the winding alleyways like a man a fourth his age. Driven on by an inward impulse that he didn't quite understand but felt compelled to obey, he rushed toward the temple. Inwardly, he presumed the Lord simply wanted him to change the location of his praying. Rounding one more corner, he saw the temple come into view. With his goal in sight, he slowed his pace to catch his breath.

Just down the street, the small family came upon another kiosk. This time, Joseph rummaged in his bag for more and larger coins. "A lamb, please," he asked this seller. "It is for the redemption of my firstborn Son," he proudly explained. This time, he shot a glance of joy mingled with pride toward his wife. They both smiled as he took the lamb up in his arms and gathered up the small cage that contained the turtledoves.

They trudged on toward the temple, but now with more life in their steps. Soon, they would dedicate their Son to the Lord—their Firstborn would now be set apart and holy to the Lord.

Joseph was relieved to mount the last step leading upward to the temple courts, as was Mary with the Babe in her arms. Feeling a bit winded, they maneuvered through the people filling the Court of the Gentiles. Their eyes scanned the premises, seeking just where they needed to go to present their offerings and receive Mary's cleansing and their Child's redemption.

By now, Simeon had found a quiet place to the side where he could pray—with his eyes open, of course. If praying with his eyes shut was the need of the moment, he could have done that just as well in his room. No, he had a clear sense that the Lord led him to the temple to show him something, or Someone.

He scanned the people as they milled about and came and went through these outer courts of the temple. They all, for the most part, looked alike. He'd been to the temple a thousand times; he saw nothing out of the ordinary today.

"Lord," he prayed, "why did You send me here so abruptly? What am I to hear or see or do here right now?"

Then, a flash of inward knowing arose within him. It was a knowing so certain that, while one cannot explain it, one need not justify it—he simply knew. There they were. There *He* was! Simeon, even if under interrogation, could not have explained how he knew, he only knew that he knew. This was Him, the One worthy of all waiting.

Joseph and Mary, their little Baby, and three sacrificial animals were doing their best to make their way through the flow of people coming and going through the courts. Joseph nearly lost the lamb from his arms once when someone wasn't watching where they were going, and then someone bumped the tiny cage so hard, he thought the turtledoves would be fluttering away when he got his head turned around. But all remained together, and they moved forward in anticipation and devotion.

Simeon, for his part, initiated his own jostling as he plowed through the crowd like a man on a mission. He kept his eyes fixed upon the couple and their Child as he mindlessly offered, "Pardon me!" "Excuse me!" "I'm sorry" to each person he knocked off their course.

Then, not fast enough but quicker than he was ready for, he stood before them—beaming!

"Hello!" he blurted abruptly.

"Hello," Joseph responded hesitantly as Mary looked up to read his face.

"Um, I'm sorry," Simeon offered. "I, um, I . . . could I hold your Baby?" he said awkwardly.

"Excuse me?" Joseph replied in surprise, but too slowly. For the old man had already snatched the child from His mother's arms before Joseph could empty his of the sacrificial animals. Mary shot a look of fear toward her husband.

"Oh! Oh! It's *You!*" the aged one exclaimed with a countenance that shone with a joy pent up so long that its release seemed it would burn his face.

The look now exchanged between mother and father was one less of fear than of confusion.

"Who are you?" Joseph asked.

"Oh! Oh! It is *You!*" the old man said again, ignoring Joseph's inquiry.

Joseph started to protest as he moved to hand off the animals to his wife, but as he opened his mouth, he heard the old man break into what seemed to be a prayer.

"At last, Lord! Now you can dismiss your servant in peace, just like you promised! With my own two eyes I have beheld your salvation—a salvation made ready for all people—a Light to shine truth upon all the peoples of the earth and to bring glory to your people Israel."[29]

With that, the old man squeezed the Child to his chest, leaned his head back toward Heaven, and said as much with his countenance as he had with his voice.

Ecstasy! That's the word that came to Mary's mind as she watched this elderly stranger adore her Son. Both father and mother sensed they had been caught up in a holy moment, though the reason for its holiness and happiness was not yet clear to them. Thus they paused—sensing no danger to their Child—and watched in wonder.

The crowds continued to bustle past them on every side, but there in the midst of the temple courts, they'd been enveloped in a bubble of worship, spotlighted in a beam of heavenly sunshine. As if a Divine finger had reached out and gently pressed a pause button inviting them to see and think and feel at a depth and in a dimension that could only be called otherworldly.

The old man lowered his head and opened his eyes, fixing them upon Mary and Joseph with an intensity that might have felt intimidating if

---

29   Luke 2:29-32

not for the love with which it was infused. Then he spoke. His words were simple enough, but they seemed freighted with an authority that arose from somewhere beyond himself. The words fell upon the parents like some odd mixture of a trumpet blast and a whispered secret.

"Look! See! Observe!" the white-haired prophet began. "This child"—he slightly elevated the child above their heads in his loving, extended arms—"is among us by God's own hand! He is present among us to fulfill a Divine destiny."

His words stirred within both mother and father a recollection of the strange events that had come upon them from the time of Mary's conception. Angel visitations. Elizabeth's prophecy. Shepherd's worship.

The old prophet continued, "God has set Him among us to bring both the hope of everlasting life and the reality of eternal judgment. On Him, the eternal destiny of every human rests."

But the old man was not yet done. "This Boy will become a Man Who will draw a line in the sand of humanity, dividing people one from another. All must decide am I with Him or am I against Him?"

Joseph gulped as Mary's brow furrowed in bewildered pain.

Then, looking deeply into Mary's eyes, the old man prophesied, "A sword will pierce through your own soul also. This son of your love will become the pain of your heart."[30]

Her eyes welled with tears.

Then the aged prophet closed his oracle. "This boy is a light, from God! He is a light that will expose the reality of all people's hearts. For this some will love Him. For this some will hate Him."

With that, the aged one turned his eyes back onto the Child. The Babe reached out His tiny hand and laid hold on the old man's downy

---

30 Luke 2:35

white beard, playfully grabbing a handful of the whiskers and pulling him near. Simeon hugged the Child close once more, then with great care delivered Him back into His mother's arms.

Jaws slack and still speechless, Mary and Joseph watched as this stranger withdrew into the crowds, melding into the mass of humanity, soon out of their sight. Neither of them was sure just how long they stood there in silence, mentally fidgeting to piece together all the events that seemed to cluster around their Boy. Their hearts sought a coherent picture of what it all could mean. As the eyes of their hearts strained to make out that picture, the weight of waiting settled even more heavily upon them.

Eventually, Joseph regathered the turtledoves and tracked down the lamb. Mary joined his side with Jesus in her arms. They moved forward to seal in worship the things that had now been freighted upon their hearts and to cast their burden upon the Lord, waiting for the outworking of His great plan for their Son.

Somewhere down one of Jerusalem's winding back alleys, a tall, lean, old man found his door, ascended the stairs he'd climbed an untold number of times, and entered the sanctuary of his tiny room. Once again, he knelt. He sighed deeply, contentedly. The weight of his long-suffered waiting dropped from his soul in a rapturous exchange of prayer. And with a smile spread across his face, Simeon fell forward to prostrate himself before God as he had so many times before. Only this time, before his face hit the floor, his now-lightened spirit was gone . . . being found immediately in the presence of the One he had sought so earnestly throughout his earthly life.

THE SCRIBE WHO
MUST BE RIGHT

IN THE DIM LIGHT EMANATING from his small oil lamp, Moshe poured over the ancient scroll unfurled before him. He rocked his head side to side in an attempt to chase away the stiffness in his neck. He paused to rub his eyes, the sting beneath his clenched eyelids reminding him of his wife Sosh's warning that if he didn't take a break now and then, he'd end up blind.

And if you are blind, her shrill voice echoed in his head, *how will you continue crafting the leather goods that pay the bills?*

Like most scribes, Moshe wasn't able to fully support himself and his family from the income he gained by teaching. The leather shop was the real breadwinner, to be sure, but it had never been his true passion. The ancient scrolls had always sat upon the throne of his heart and played in the fields of his mind.

Heeding the inaudible voice of his beloved, Moshe rocked back in his seat for a moment. Allowing the breezes of a mental pause to blow through his mind, he felt his thoughts stray back to his childhood home in Asibla, a small village that lay along the northeasterly road between Damascus and Palmyra.

flash back

79

As a result of the diaspora, his family had lived as part of a minority Jewish population. For some, the immersion in a Gentile culture was a lure away from strict faithfulness to God and His Law, but not for Moshe's family.

His father, a good Jewish man, had instructed his sons at home. He worked tirelessly with them to memorize portions of the Torah. He assiduously drilled them in the language of God—the written Hebrew language. After all, had it not been the very finger of God that had written the Ten Commandments on the stone tablets on Mount Sinai?

Moshe could still hear his father's deep, resonate voice as he led them in reciting portions of Holy Scripture. He and his brothers had learned well, but Moshe clearly stood out among them. They wanted to honor God, but Moshe wanted to master God's words—to internalize the will of the Lord until there was no guessing as to what would please Him. Had his father foreseen this drive in Moshe? Or had he planted and nurtured it within him? After all, he had named him Moshe, after the great Lawgiver, Moses. Or, technically, the great Law-*receiver*.

As he grew, Moshe had gone to the synagogue for further, more technical instruction. Here, too, Moshe's star shone brighter than the rest—not so much in skill, though he had that, but in passion and drive. The others certainly did not depreciate God's Law, but Moshe revered it beyond all comparison. He soon outpaced the other students. It wasn't long before the local scribes were murmuring among themselves about Moshe's facility with the language, the capacity of his memory, the insightfulness of his interpretations, and the sagacity of the applications he drew from the text of Scripture.

But a big fish in a small pond never really knows what it's like to swim in the ocean. Moshe could win every debate in the synagogue in Asibla, but what if he were in Jerusalem? Would he always be right there?

One evening, as the family broke bread together, Moshe's father had lifted his voice in a tone that always meant he was about to announce something to which he had devoted much thought. This meant, of course, that the matter was already settled; and though his father never seemed to be laying down the law, the family knew that once he had spoken, there would be no further discussion.

Turning and fixing his eyes upon Moshe, his father announced that he had arranged for Moshe to study in Jerusalem in a prominent synagogue under the direction of some of the best scribes the Hebrew nation had to offer.

Silence enveloped the room. His mother wept. They were tears of joy over a son who had proven so zealous for the Torah of the Lord, but they were mingled with sadness as well for the separation this would bring. Her Moshe would be alone in that great city!

One of Moshe's brothers rested a hand on his shoulder in a gesture that communicated both congratulations and honor. Two others bobbed their heads up and down in a silent acknowledgement of what had already been clear to them all—Moshe was the pride of the family, and this opportunity was his due.

Moshe himself was awash in a myriad of emotions. Joy: *Me, in Jerusalem! Studying with the scribes in the capital city!* Fear: *Will I be seen to be a fool? Can I prove that I can handle the Torah rightly?* Sadness: *How will I ever survive without my family?*

Soon, Moshe had found himself wandering the streets he'd seen only once before, during a pilgrimage with his father. He was no longer the prized pupil, but at least he was there. No one else from his village or the entire region where he grew up had ever gotten this far!

But gnawing, fear-filled questions kept chewing away at the fringes of his conscious thoughts: *Can I do this? Do I know enough? Will I be proven wrong?*

As the months unfolded, Moshe battled his fears with the weapon of increased effort. He studied harder than ever. He determined that no student would outwork him. And it showed. His instructors silently took notice. They didn't say it, but he could feel it. Moshe was moving up.

Yet, inwardly, in a silent place that others could not see, something had changed within Moshe. He didn't see it yet himself. He was too absorbed in his work. But Moshe's passion for the Law had become, in a subtle but dangerous shift of emphasis, a zeal to be right. Not just to be upright. Not just to be righteous. But to be *right*. He was driven to have the answer, always. Without fail, his must be the correct answer. He simply had to be the one in the right, whatever else was said or argued. He longed for the right answer; to possess the right answer; to intone it, for it to be heard on *his* lips.

The answer to what? To anything! To everything! The necessity to be ready with the authoritative answer to whatever may come became the unspoken, unexamined reason for Moshe's existence. Gravitas can be its own kind of idol.

In the name of all that is right, something decidedly unrighteous had been planted in Moshe's soul. An unseen hand was tilling and tending and watering and nurturing it. Moshe was changing.

Then came the day when Moshe was finally given his robes. *The robes!* The long, flowing robes, otherwise restricted to nobility, were attainable by those of non-noble blood in only one way—through scholarship, through study, through being quick with the correct answer—by always being *right*. Moshe had dreamed of this day for years, but learning to enjoy those robes took only a moment. It was a pleasure of which one never really spoke, but secretly, he cherished it as a private indulgence. He gloried in the way his robes rippled in the breeze as he made his way through the streets. The colors, the pattern, the material—they all set him off as an accomplished scribe. The deference he felt coming from the doorways would have been even more intoxicating had he not felt that it was his just due, his right for being right. Regularly, consistently, reliably, unfailingly, always right—this was his ticket to respect. The sound of the fabric's snap in a strong wind served as a herald announcing his coming to those who owed him their admiration. These robes were his security clearance and free ticket to any front row seat, and most importantly, to reserved seats in the synagogue. Being right was his invitation to lead in prayer at civic and religious events. And how he relished the opportunity to hear his voice ring out in the synagogue while all others quietly listened.

But the greatest honor of all was to be called Rabbi.

More and more, in situation after situation, Moshe had become the voice of authority. The days of responding to questions from his teachers were behind him now, and the people were increasingly seeking from him answers to their questions about God's Law and will. But though Moshe spoke of God's Law, it was *his* word that became law. It wasn't just what God had said, but what Moshe said about what God said. After all, as the rabbis had written, "It is more punishable to act against the words of the Scribes than those of Scripture."

Moshe wasn't above his teachers yet—and they periodically let him know it—but he was rising. This they all knew.

Now Moshe, still seated at his desk, was called from his memories by the sound of his wife clearing her throat dramatically. Raising his head, he was met with a look from her suggesting that not only too much studying would keep him from feeding the family, but also too much remembering.

One quiet afternoon as Moshe was absorbed in his work, poring over a scroll of Micah the prophet, a courier burst into the synagogue, shattering the stillness. Heads popped up from manuscripts, and wide eyes were soon studying the intruder. Through gasps for air, the Gentile messenger revealed that Herod was urgently requesting that a panel of the best scribes be immediately gathered to his presence.

The emissary had arrived in off hours, so they weren't able to assemble the best scribes. Lemeck was missing, and no one seemed to know just where he was at the moment. Moshe stood quietly off to the side, wondering what was unfolding before him. With a quick nod and a call of command, his superiors told him to join the party. They despised Herod, but they dared not delay him. So out the door they went, rushing through the streets toward the Fortress of Antonia, which served as headquarters for Herod as he governed the province for the Romans.

It was an odd scene—a Roman herald racing over the cobblestone in Jerusalem followed by a gaggle of bookish scribes. Scribes don't run! They *glide!*

As they huffed through the streets on their way to the Fortress, their minds reeled with questions. *Herod? Why would he wish to see us? What could this mean?* And a good dose of fear mingled with their curiosity.

Decades before, Herod had been named king of the Jews by Octavius Caesar. But he was no Jew—at least not a pure Jew. It was common knowledge that he was a half-breed Idumean. Yes, he had built the magnificent temple in Jerusalem, and there were those who said this was proof of his legitimacy and a passion for God. But others saw in this little more than political pandering, for had he not also installed a Roman eagle over the gate to the temple of God? Was it not at his command that other temples were built to pagan gods? Had he not, over the years, taken ten wives? And beyond all this, there was blood on the man's hands—much blood! And not just that which comes in times of war, but the blood of innocents, including that of one of his wives and several of his sons.

As they rounded a corner in the narrow street, the rising towers of Antonia came into view. Racing up the steps, they took note of the centurions lining the way and the glint of their well-polished weapons. As they disappeared into an interior hallway, the Roman slowed his pace and exhorted the scribes to catch their breath and ready themselves before entering Herod's presence. They all took a moment to inhale deeply, straighten their robes, and compose their thoughts. Then, they were standing before the man who staunchly declared himself king of the Jews. The sparkle and sheen of the chamber and the size and demeanor of the guards added to the awe that swept over the scribes.

Moshe's role here was simply to be a body, to fill a spot, to be a number whose presence made their collective whole appear more official. The head of the synagogue had whispered in his ear as they raced through the streets, "Just keep your mouth shut; let us senior scribes do the talking!" That's all Moshe had to do. Just stand there and try not to shake. And above all, *don't speak.*

When Moshe finally laid eyes upon Herod, he found him not what he had expected. Nearly seventy years of age and in increasingly ill health, the king wore a worn and anxious countenance. And something sinister seemed to be brewing behind his bulging eyes.

The awkward silence was broken when the official standing to Herod's right raised his voice to thank them for coming on such short notice. Moshe thought to himself that Herod looked anything but grateful, but that line of thought was cut short by what the official said next.

"Your king would like to know from you, who have spent your lives scouring the Word of God, where the Christ is to be born."

The question hung in the air. A couple of the scribes' Adam's apples bobbed up and down in their throats as they swallowed in nervousness. The chief cast his eyes to the floor. *Why,* they each wondered, *would Herod be asking us* this?

The silence lasted but a moment, yet it seemed much longer than that to Moshe. These were men who had given their all to know the Word of God so thoroughly that they could answer without hesitation any question put to them. To Moshe, the silence that followed felt like a humiliating sign of incompetence.

Herod, whose eyes had been resting in a distracted gaze upon a nondescript point on the floor, slowly raised them to lock on these Jewish men of the Book. The temperature in the room seemed to spike, and the pressure to answer rose dramatically.

It was clear now that the rumors that had filled the streets of Jerusalem over the last few days had been true. Several days before, strangely dressed travelers from the East—Magi or "wise men"—had wandered into the city. They had come, they said, under the guidance of a star. As the story went, they had made their way to Herod's court and asked, "Where is He who has been born King of the Jews?"[31] They had come, they said, to worship this new King.

Little wonder Herod wasn't in a festive mood. He reckoned that the Jews already had a king, and he was not interested in surrendering his throne.

The awkwardness of his associates' silence was more than Moshe could take. *Why don't you say something?* They were stalling, trying to figure out just what Herod's angle was and what the safest answer would be.

Moshe, on his part, mistook their silence for ignorance. *Maybe it's the pressure,* he thought. *They've all frozen under the stress!*

But not Moshe; he had the answer immediately. He knew it. He had been, providentially, hovering over the scroll of Micah at the very moment Herod's courier had come crashing into the synagogue.

Moshe's mind reeled in confusion. Not over the answer—that he knew, and he knew that he was right. *But,* he desperately wondered, *should I say something?* He recalled the unambiguous nature of the command the senior scribe had issued. *But,* Moshe thought, *our*

---

31   Matthew 2:2

silence is humiliating. We look stupid! Incompetent! How can this glorify the
Law of the Lord?

And then, suddenly, Moshe heard his own voice. He did not recall
making a decision to speak. But he heard himself blurting out in
response, "In Bethlehem of Judea, for so it is written by the prophet:
'And you, O Bethlehem, in the land of Judah, are by no means least
among the rulers of Judah; for from you shall come a ruler who will
shepherd my people Israel.'"[32]

And just like that, the hall fell silent again. The awkwardness
continued, but it was different now. Moshe could feel the angry
stares of the other scribes boring holes in the side of his head. But
worst of all was the sinister expression that washed over Herod's face.
When Moshe had come to the words "from you shall come a ruler,"
the king had risen slowly to a standing position.

The man at Herod's right hand hastily dismissed the party of
scribes, perfunctorily thanking them for their time.

Just as swiftly as they found themselves in Herod's chamber, they
were alone in the street again, just outside Antonia.

The verbal assault from the other scribes began immediately.
The most senior among them drew himself up till his nose nearly
touched Moshe's. In bitter tones with spittle flying and left hanging
from his beard, he said, "Didn't I tell you to keep your mouth shut?"

The others joined in:

"Don't you realize what you've done?"

"Did you see the look in his eyes?"

"Haven't you heard what he's done to his own family?"

---

32   Matthew 2:5-6

"What do you think the parents of Bethlehem would say to you right now?"

"Did you even think about the consequences of your answer?"

Moshe felt his face flush.

Moshe hadn't thought of *that*. All he had thought of was being correct, of having the right answer. And his answer *was* correct and right . . . Wasn't it?

Something one of the scribes said echoed in his mind for some time after that day. "Truth can be used as a weapon as well as a balm." Sadly, Herod had established a pretty clear record of what he was willing to do with the truth.

The next twenty-four hours were torturously long for all of them, but especially for Moshe.

With the next dawn came the news from Bethlehem. Under the cover of night Herod's troops had descended upon the unsuspecting village. Every baby boy under two was killed. Barely a home in Bethlehem was left that was not touched by the grizzly aftermath of Herod's jealousy.

As Moshe sat silently in the synagogue filled with those gathered to mourn the loss, the words of Jeremiah the prophet ran through his mind: "A voice was heard in Ramah, weeping and loud lamentation, Rachel weeping for her children; she refused to be comforted, because they are no more."[33]

Yes, he had gotten the reference right, but he had been so very wrong.

Heartbroken and guilt-ridden, Moshe longed for the simpler, quieter days of his childhood in Asibla. Growing up there, he'd longed

---

33 Jeremiah 31:15

for the streets of Jerusalem. But now, with the blood of many babies on his hands, he could only wish for home.

In the aftermath of it all, Moshe nearly quit. But instead, he filled the hours and weeks and months and years to come in what had always been his comfort—poring over the sacred texts of the Law, the Prophets, and the Writings. But now as he did so, a dark, unrelenting shade had settled over his heart.

He had been right. But he also knew that he had been wrong.

He lingered more and more over those words of Jeremiah the prophet. As the years passed, he calculated the ages of the boys from Bethlehem and imagined what they might have done that day, had they still been alive.

And he held fast to a wisp of gossip that had filtered back into town in the weeks after the infanticide. It was said that a child and his family had slipped out of Bethlehem just moments before Herod's men had arrived. It was almost, they said, as if they had known what was coming and had been rushed out of town and down the road by an unseen hand.

Moshe took some solace in this thought: *one child; at least there was one.* Yet still, he tortured himself: *If only the others . . .*

Then one day, in the midst of his despair, a Scripture descended to his conscious thoughts like down wafting on a gentle breeze: "Out of Egypt I called my son."[34] *Hmm,* Moshe thought, *I wonder why that came to mind. What's that got to do with anything?*

Year melded into year, and Moshe's career recovered from the great blunder in Antonia. The senior scribe had passed a few years after that, and the others seemed not to hold it against him. After all, it always was the first impulse of a scribe to be right.

Then, one day a decade or so later, as Moshe wandered into the temple courts, he observed a crowd of scribes huddled around something. As he approached, he couldn't see what was happening, so he found something to stand on and peered over the huddled mass. To his amazement, they circled a boy who appeared to be no more than twelve years of age. The boy was fielding their questions! It was the role of the scribe to take the questions of the common man and to provide the correct answers. It was they who did the educating. No wonder a crowd had gathered!

As Moshe listened in, he realized why the scribes were thunderstruck by this child. His answers were like none he had ever heard.

When the boy's mother eventually pulled him away to take him home, it was over the complaints of the scribes. As the crowd broke up, Moshe grabbed a fellow scribe he recognized.

"Who was that boy?" he asked.

"I don't know. He said his name was Jesus."

"Where is he from?" Moshe demanded.

"Don't know that either. Could be almost anywhere, I suppose. You know the crowds we've had here for the Passover."

Moshe wandered away, deep in thought. The words of the eighth Psalm ran through his mind: "Out of the mouth of infants and nursing babies you have prepared praise."[35] He wondered to himself, *I've spent a lifetime learning the Scriptures. How can a boy so young know them so well?*

---

35   Psalm 8:2; Matthew 21:16

As the years rolled by, Moshe began to think of this boy in connection with the lost children of Bethlehem: *What has become of the boy who escaped? Could he be the prodigy in the temple?* Those and other questions often filled his mind as he lay upon his mat at night before sleep overtook him.

Then Moshe would dream. Sometimes, there were great debates in which he always proved right in the end. Sometimes, he endured nightmares of blood on his hands that no soap could wash away. Sometimes, he saw himself standing before the bar of God, and, despite having all the right answers, he knew he needed more than right answers; he needed to *be* right in the Lord's sight. But he wasn't.

Decades swept by, and soon most of a lifetime stood behind Moshe. Now aged, he had risen to prominence in Jerusalem. Asibla and childhood were faint memories. His family was gone. He was no longer the small-town diaspora Jew whom others suspected was tainted by the Hellenization of the culture. No, he had achieved his dream. But the dream had not delivered what he'd imagined it would.

Yes, he knew the answers. And yes, people respected him. The robes were still a nice perk. The front row seats and the special greetings were a pleasure well hidden beneath expressions of spiritual seriousness. But for all the rightness of his religion, he was a man haunted by memories of a day in Herod's court and the night that followed in Bethlehem.

He had learned to distract himself most of the time. For example, lately there had been the diversion of trying to figure out the latest sensation to capture the imagination of the people. A new rabbi from—can you imagine?—Galilee had burst onto the scene. He was, by most estimations, something of a radical. He wasn't connected with any single synagogue. He hadn't signed on with the Pharisaic party, but he wasn't a Sadducee either. He was, Moshe had concluded, a third-party rabbi—just the kind that made everybody nervous.

Periodically the Rabbi—Who Moshe now learned was named Jesus—would appear in Jerusalem. Crowds would always gather. Several times, Moshe had stood on the fringe and listened to Him teach. Clearly, He'd not been schooled in proper pedagogy. He didn't quote or footnote the rabbis. His words didn't seem practiced, but they flowed freely from somewhere deep inside Himself. His words possessed a self-authenticating quality. It reminded Moshe of someone, but he couldn't quite call up the memory.

A few times, Moshe wanted to argue a point with the Rabbi, but he held his peace. He'd learned long ago that wisdom is often found not in being the first to speak, but the last.

Moshe did speak to Him one day, however, when he saw the Rabbi in the temple court. Several in the crowd were pressing a point with him. Moshe wandered over and heard the incompetence of those debating the Rabbi. He thought this might be his chance, so he raised his voice over the din and directed a question toward the Rabbi. "Which commandment is the most important of all?"[36]

Immediately, the younger Man answered, "The most important is, 'Hear, O Israel: The Lord our God, the Lord is one. And you shall love the Lord your God with all your heart and with all your soul and with all your mind and with all your strength.'"[37]

---

36   Matthew 22:36
37   Matthew 22:37

Ah, yes, Moshe thought. *Good answer.* Before he could form his next question, he heard the young Teacher continue. "The second is this: 'You shall love your neighbor as yourself.' There is no other commandment greater than these."[38]

"Yes!" Moshe found himself saying. "You are right, Teacher. You have truly said that he is one, and there is no other besides him. And to love him with all the heart and with all the understanding and with all the strength, and to love one's neighbor as oneself, is much more than all whole burnt offerings and sacrifices."[39]

There, thought Moshe. *I've established the playing field. He's obviously a man of intelligence, and I've given him a passing grade. He'll surely be grateful for my authentication of his ministry.*

As Moshe turned to go, the Rabbi called out after him: "You are not far from the kingdom of God."[40]

Moshe froze mid-stride. Someone in the crowd gasped. Moshe was both embarrassed and a bit outraged. *Had this young Man the audacity to render a verdict upon him, a respected scribe and rabbi? Did He think He was in a position to determine whether Moshe was right?*

Fleeing the awkwardness, the crowd filtered away, and Moshe decided to join them. From that point on, no one dared to ask the young Rabbi any more questions.

Some time passed before Moshe bothered to listen to any more of this man's teaching. But that didn't mean it wasn't on his mind. *The audacity! The arrogance!*

Then one day, he again caught the sound of the Rabbi's voice above the noise at the temple. Moshe drew near, making sure to stay

---

38   Matthew 22:39
39   Mark 12:32-33
40   Mark 12:34

at the edge of the crowd. As the Rabbi made His point, Moshe lifted up his voice, knowing it would be heard, but also that it couldn't be pinned on him while he was hidden in the crowds.

"Teacher, you have spoken well."[41]

Ha! Moshe thought. *That'll teach him!*

But the young Rabbi addressed the crowd yet again. "How can they say that the Christ is David's son?"[42]

There was an awkward silence. Then the Rabbi continued, "For David himself says in the Book of Psalms, 'The Lord said to my Lord, Sit at my right hand, until I make your enemies your footstool.'" The Teacher paused for dramatic effect and then drove home His point. "David thus calls him Lord, so how is he his son?"[43]

Again, silence enveloped the crowd. The scribes present pondered their sandal straps, unable to think of anything to say in reply.

Dumbstruck, Moshe's mind reeled: *What! Wait, I . . . no . . . uh . . . what? What did He say? Why have I never seen that before?* And with that he, too, was lost in a silent search for an answer.

The Rabbi then turned to His own disciples and in a voice loud enough for all the crowd to clearly make out, warned, "Beware of the scribes, who like to walk around in long robes, and love greetings in the marketplaces and the best seats in the synagogues and the places of honor at feasts, who devour widows' houses and for a pretense make long prayers. They will receive the greater condemnation."[44]

Oh, that's it! Moshe thought. *Enough! Someone has to put an end to this nonsense.* He stormed off to figure out how that might be accomplished.

---

41   Luke 20:39
42   Luke 20:41
43   Luke 20:41-44
44   Luke 20:46-47

Moshe fumed for weeks. And the more he thought about it, the angrier he became. There were official motions introduced at scribal meetings to the effect that they should take collective action against this rabbi. A lynching fever grew as the celebration of Passover drew near.

There was something in Moshe that resonated with the sentiments and intentions of his fellow scribes. But in the last few weeks, his dreams had also become more unsettling. They were still about dead baby boys and occasionally about the boy in the temple. But more prevalent now were the nightmares of standing before God and hearing the statutes of the Law read against him. And every time, Moshe was left speechless. He had no answer. He knew what the right answer was—that he was not right with God—but he couldn't *speak* it. He just couldn't form the words. And there was the clear awareness that though he had the right answer, to have spoken it would have been to condemn himself.

Each time he awakened in a cold sweat, gasping for air.

Moshe had spent a lifetime in pursuit of being right, but he was increasingly troubled by the thought that he should have been more concerned with being right with God.

And his thoughts—what was going on with them? The young rabbi had rightly said that the scribes "sit on Moses' seat."[45] They are, after all, the official interpreters of what God meant when He gave Moses the Law. But this Rabbi, though a Teacher, was more. He spoke with authority, as would a prophet. He spoke not just as a prophet, but as one would expect *the* Prophet to speak.

Surely not! No, this just couldn't be right!

---

45   Matthew 23:2

Yet Moses himself had said, "The Lord your God will raise up for you a prophet like me from among you, from your brothers—it is to him you shall listen."[46]

Moshe didn't like where his thoughts were leading him. In fact, he'd spent a great deal of energy resisting them—but the question kept returning to his mind. *If the Prophet like Moses did come, would He speak any differently than this Man?*

As the days drew near for the Passover celebration, an increasingly tortured Moshe pulled back from the front lines of ministry. His scribe brothers were out in full regalia. But Moshe just couldn't do it. Something within held him back. Was it holy wrath or a guilty conscience? The two had become so entwined over the years, he wasn't sure which was what. He didn't trust himself anymore. And a scribe who couldn't trust himself to be right wasn't much help to anyone, was he?

Moshe spent the days until Passover in fasting and prayer, calling upon God for some kind of light that would end his misery and for a peace that would quell his decades-old guilt.

He wasn't there on Thursday evening when the Sanhedrin officially voted to hunt down the Rabbi and bring Him in. He wasn't present for the events of the following hours. But every detail was reported to him.

During the night, Moshe, unable to sleep, unfurled the scroll of Isaiah and spread it out on the table. Hour after hour, he pored over it. *What did the Prophet mean? Of Whom did He speak?*

Every line seemed filled with an ocean of meaning, frustratingly obscured by a dense fog that lay over Moshe's heart. Of everything he read, one line drew him back again and again: "When his soul makes an offering for guilt . . . the righteous one, my servant, will make many to be accounted righteous."[47]

How could that be? Didn't David himself say, "No one living is righteous before you"?[48]

Moshe had given his years and vitality to being someone who was always unfailingly right. But he wasn't. That much he knew.

In desperation, as if fleeing from an unseen accuser, Moshe ripped himself away from the scroll and rushed out the door and down the street. *I need air! I've got to clear my head! Maybe I am losing my mind . . .*

As he hastened down a side street in search of solitude, he stumbled upon the exact opposite. At the first intersection, he met a crowd that was unusually large, even for festival time. He was about to whirl and return the way he came when he saw Him—the Teacher, the Rabbi. He was bloodied, beaten, stumbling under the weight of a heavy cross.

A passage from the Isaiah scroll ran through his mind: "His appearance was so marred, beyond human semblance, and his form beyond that of the children of mankind."[49]

Then he heard some mocker in the crowd call out the Teacher's name—Jesus.

Jesus! No, couldn't be. I mean, it's a common enough name, but . . .

He now realized just who this Rabbi had been making him think of. *How did I not make this connection before?* A boy in the temple, so long ago, the Boy with the right answers. *Could it be?*

Then, by a mysterious power he did not recognize but seemed helpless to resist, he recalled something he'd heard this Jesus say to a crowd in the temple. "Every scribe who has been trained for the kingdom of heaven is like a master of a house, who brings out of his treasure what is new and what is old."[50]

The shouts of derision rising from the crowd now caught Moshe's attention, and again, Isaiah came to him. "He was despised and rejected by men; a man of sorrows, and acquainted with grief; and as one from whom men hide their faces he was despised, and we esteemed him not."[51]

The words from the Isaiah scroll continued to involuntarily tumble through his mind as he joined the throng following behind Jesus.

Motionless at the fringe of the crowd, Moshe heard the thud of the cross hit the ground and the groan that arose as Jesus was thrust upon it. He heard the sickening thud of the hammer against the spikes as Jesus was fixed to the beam. Again, the inescapable voice in his head said, "He was wounded for our transgressions; he was crushed for our iniquities; upon him was the chastisement that brought us peace."[52]

When the cross was dropped in the hole prepared for it, the voice within his heart rose up again. "With his stripes we are healed."

Some of his fellow scribes approached the cross and hurled venomous accusations toward Jesus as He hung there dying.

"He saved others," they shouted. "He cannot save himself!"[53]

Moshe could not join them. His thoughts swirled in a vortex that pulled down from Heaven the words of God that he had treasured for a lifetime. *The Prophets! The Psalms! The Law of Moses!* At the same time, they were both a voice of condemnation and a light shining in a dark place, beckoning him to come and find peace.

---

50   Matthew 13:52
51   Isaiah 53:3
52   Isaiah 53:5
53   Matthew 27:42

And then, an audible Voice broke into his thoughts. It was the Voice of the Rabbi. From the cross, He prayed, "Father, forgive them, for they know not what they do."[54]

No sooner did the Teacher's voice trail off than Moshe heard the words of Isaiah again within his heart. "He was cut off out of the land of the living, stricken for the transgression of my people."[55]

Jesus spoke again a bit later, this time to one of those crucified with Him. "Truly, I say to you, today you will be with me in Paradise."[56] An echo of Isaiah came again to Moshe: "There was no deceit in his mouth."[57]

Sometime later, taking up David's own call, Jesus cried out, "My God, my God, why have you forsaken me?"[58]

In the silence that enveloped the crowd, Moshe heard Isaiah's words: "The Lord has laid on him the iniquity of us all."[59]

Eventually, Jesus gathered up all his strength and cried out, "It is finished!"[60]

By now, Moshe was anticipating Isaiah's words to enter his mind, and sure enough, they did. "His soul makes an offering for guilt."[61]

Finally, Jesus prayed, "Father, into your hands I commit my spirit."[62]

Then Moshe heard his own voice. Just as in the Fortress of Antonia about thirty years before, he didn't remember making a decision to speak. He simply heard himself praying.

54 Luke 23:34
55 Isaiah 53:8
56 Luke 23:43
57 Isaiah 53:9
58 Psalm 22:1; Matthew 27:46
59 Isaiah 53:6
60 John 19:30
61 Isaiah 53:10
62 Luke 23:46

"Yes, Father," Moshe whispered. "Me, too. Into your hands I commit *my* spirit, my whole life."

Then he realized that Jesus was dead.

Not everyone noticed immediately. There was too much mocking and reviling. One of the criminals crucified with Jesus was still crying out. But Moshe noticed, and one final time, the words of Isaiah the prophet came to him. "The righteous one, my servant, will make many to be accounted righteous."[63]

Moshe couldn't remember a midday so dark, yet he'd also never experienced such light inside his mind and heart.

Jesus—He was *the* Righteous One. He was the *only* Righteous One. On that fateful day, the Lord had laid Moshe's iniquities upon his innocent Son and judged them there. The Father had taken Jesus' life instead of Moshe's. In an epic reversal of standard accounting practices, Jesus' own righteousness had caused Moshe to be "counted righteous" by God.

Though he'd spent a lifetime seeking to be right, now, for the first time, he knew what it felt like to be made right—to be declared righteous by God and to be at peace with Him.

---

63   Isaiah 53:11

CUSTOM-MADE

THE ACRID-SWEET SCENT OF FRESH sawdust both pleased his senses and tickled his sinuses. The combination was just enough to evoke a thunderous but not unpleasant sneeze. This had become a familiar morning ritual to Gamal, who loved the feel of his tiny woodshop. The smells were only part of the joy. His heart always warmed at the moment when the sun broke through the window to expose the particulate floating lazily through the room. The worn-but-ready tools fit his hands like custom-made gloves. The rustle of the curtains in the breeze, the way the sounds made their way through the walls from the street outside—it all combined to make this *home*. But it was more than just home; to Gamal, it was almost a holy place, a temple where the sacrifice of his labor was applied with devotion to something that mattered.

Gamal only wished he could find Someone to whom it could be lifted as a worthy offering. Gamal had been searching his entire life for this as-yet-unidentified, nameless One. Not that his life was completely empty—his parents were all he could ask for. They had always supported and encouraged him. They had so instilled the valuable lessons of honor, community, unselfishness, and the sanctity of one's labor that they stood like weight-bearing pillars in Gamal's heart. His wife, Rania, was a jewel—hardworking, devoted, faithful, a wonderful mother. And his children! His son, Nour, and daughter, Nubia, were the gleam in his eye and the song in his heart.

Yet there remained in Gamal a settled yearning that was unfulfilled to this day. As good as his lineage and family was, as much as he cherished his trade, there was still a void inside him.

The sun god, Ra, was born each morning in the east and sent rays of light through the window, exposing to Gamal's eyes what the darkness had hidden. But it could not chase away the darkness of his heart. All his neighbors seemed satisfied living here in On, the historic "city of the sun." (The Greeks had adapted that name when they dubbed it Heliopolis, and the Hebrews likewise called it Beth-shemesh.) But even Ra was having a hard time keeping up with the times. With the rise of Alexandria, On was a mere shadow of its former self. The temple of Ra-Atum remained, but the priesthood was scrambling for recruits. The city's renowned obelisks still drew admirers, but their visits were driven more by nostalgia than devotion. The depopulation of the city had not only called in question the people's devotion to Ra, but also his ability to save even himself. The sun still rose each day, but to Gamal, the cult of Ra seemed mired in twilight.

Gamal's spiritual struggle was like an incomplete part in one of his furniture projects. One-half of a perfectly prepared mortise-and-tenon joint had been prepared within him—and not by him, but by some unseen hand—and now simply waited for the other handcrafted half of the joint to appear one day. He longed for his life to be fitted together, finished, completed, made whole.

A rap at the door interrupted Gamal's silent reverie.

"Is this the woodworker's shop?" a deep voice inquired through the door. It was not an unfamiliar inquiry, but the question was carried by a thick, distinct accent. Not entirely foreign, but not from On.

The sturdy, handcrafted door turned smoothly on its hinges and swung open to reveal a tall, black man with a massive, muscular frame and a regal bearing. Gamal was dwarfed by his size, but the man's countenance—including a wide, brilliant smile with the whitest teeth Gamal thought he'd ever seen—radiated a kindness that put him at ease.

"Hello," Gamal offered, bowing his head in respectful deference. "I am Gamal. I am a woodworker, and this is my shop." He motioned toward the work area with a sweep of his hand.

"Wonderful!" said the giant. "I am Negasi, a servant of Candace, queen of the Ethiopians."

Gamal's eyes grew wide, and his eyebrows rose; then he responded with a deeper bow that involved not only his head but also his entire torso. "To what do I owe this honor?" he said.

"I have been on a mission for our queen, and I must soon return to her throne room. In passing through your city, I have become the guest of one of your leading priests. Last night as we dined, I could not help but admire the exquisite table at which we ate. I inquired, and he told me that you are the man who crafted this remarkable piece of furniture. I must have one just like it to present to my queen."

Gamal was again taken aback and not quite sure what to say. Finally, fumbling for words, he confessed, "Yes, I do make tables." Then he thought to ask, "Can you describe the table for me? Or perhaps it is easier if you tell me the priest's name?"

"Yes," the Ethiopian replied, "his name is Amosis."

Gamal immediately knew exactly what table the man had experienced. That's how Gamal chose to think of his furniture—not something just to be seen or used, but to be *experienced*.

The statesman asked, "Could you make me another just like it?"

Gamal nodded in consent.

"When could it be ready? How long will it take? I have been away for some time and must make my return as soon as possible."

"I do have several other orders before yours," Gamal said, "but I think I could delay most of them long enough to take on your table. But the exact time depends on several other factors, one being the availability of the materials. As I recall, I used something like five different species of wood, counting all the inlays. Another is the dimensions. Do you want it precisely the same size?"

"Yes, exactly," responded the obviously pleased servant of Candace. Then he added, "The inlay is so beautiful. Please, reproduce it as nearly as possible in my table as well. But I must say that it is the solidity of the table that most struck me. It is stable as a stone! Queen Candace will be most pleased!"

Gamal was well-known in On for his quality craftsmanship, but still, he was not used to such high praise. His eyes fell to the floor as he fumbled for appropriate words of response. Finally, he managed, "Thank you. I will begin tomorrow morning. I will do my best to hasten the project to completion, but I must tell you, I will not sacrifice quality for haste."

With that, the Ethiopian dignitary bowed and left him with his richest expressions of gratitude.

Gamal waited long enough to be certain his visitor was gone. Then he burst through the door of his shop and leaped up the steps two at a time to his family's dwelling above. He had to tell Rania and the children that he had been commissioned to build a table for a queen!

The next morning found Gamal in his sanctuary at his customary early hour. He loved the sight of the sun's first rays peeking over the building across the street and through his shop window. As the room lit, Gamal gathered several lengths of lumber and ran his hands over them. He was examining them, yes. But master craftsman that he was, Gamal communed with the wood. Each board had its own personality, a grain that had to be understood before it could be tamed, trimmed, and fitted into place in a project. Lost in his assessment, Gamal was startled when a knock came at his shop door. He jumped a bit before he heard the rich, deep, heavily accented voice of his new Ethiopian customer.

Gamal opened the door with an expression of surprise upon his face. *Oh no, I bragged to my family too soon! Negasi has come to cancel his order!*

Before he could speak, Negasi half-apologized, half-petitioned, "Would it be all right if I watch you work?"

Gamal clearly must have looked confused because Negasi immediately followed up with the words, "I love to watch a master at work, whatever his field of endeavor."

What could he say to that? He silently motioned for the imposing dignitary to enter, cleared some debris from a bench, and invited him to take a seat.

Gamal did his best to pretend he was alone, and Negasi did his best to let the master work his magic on the wood. But time and again, the visitor's curiosity got the better of him, and he kept interjecting questions, most beginning with "Why?" It didn't take long for Gamal to realize this wasn't going to work. He'd never make any headway. So, in desperation, he seized upon the strategy of asking Negasi the questions.

His first question opened a fount that flowed for some time. "Can you tell me about your most recent mission? That is, if it wasn't top-secret."

Negasi assured him it was not classified and began unfolding his itinerary—places visited, dignitaries engaged, political points scored. It was just boring enough that Gamal was finally able to concentrate on his work while half-listening to his new foreign friend.

Wood shavings flew around the room from the plane in Gamal's hand. The piece of wood he had chosen was perfect and was cooperating with his efforts. Negasi was deep into his narration. All Gamal had to do to keep the script rolling was to insert an occasional "Oh!" or "Really?" or "That's amazing!" His resonant bass voice carried on, hardly missing a beat.

Eventually, Gamal needed a drink of water and a breather. So he offered his friend a drink as well and joined him for a moment near the bench.

"So, did you enjoy your mission?" Gamal asked.

"Enjoy? Yes. But I must say that this trip has brought me something priceless, something that no amount of high-level political maneuvering, the opulence of a royal court, or name-dropping could ever afford me."

Gamal took the bait. He formed a question to accompany his quizzical expression: "Would you tell me about it?"

"I had left Jerusalem and was heading south to make my way here, by way of Gaza, and then eventually on home to Ethiopia. I was in the middle of nowhere, nothing but sand, stone, and scrub as far as

I could see. I had picked up an old scroll of Hebrew religious texts while in Jerusalem."

Sensing the need to explain, he added, "My queen likes her court to keep abreast of how our neighbors think.

"I was reading the scroll of a prophet the Hebrews call Isaiah from about six hundred years ago. I must say it doesn't read like any religious text I've ever studied. It was remarkable, but I just wasn't getting it. As I was absorbed in the text, I was startled by a man. I have no idea where he came from. I didn't think I'd gotten so lost in reading that I wasn't aware of my surroundings; but suddenly, there he was, running toward my chariot! I was startled at first, but as he approached, a bit winded, he asked, 'Do you understand what you are reading?'"[64]

Now Gamal was the one lost in thought. He urged Negasi forward, goading him with a simple "And?"

"And," the Ethiopian continued, "I said, 'How can I, unless someone guides me?'[65] He seemed eager to talk, so I invited him into the chariot. He wanted to know where precisely in the scroll I was reading."

"And?" Gamal urged him on.

"I re-read him the last few lines I'd been puzzling over before he approached."

Negasi reached behind him to retrieve his bag. "I believe I have the scroll right here," he said. Finding it and unfurling it until he located the precise spot, he then read, "'Like a sheep he was led to the slaughter and like a lamb before its shearer is silent, so he opens not his mouth. In his humiliation justice was denied him. Who can describe his generation? For his life is taken away from the earth.'[66] I stopped here,

---

64   Acts 8:30
65   Acts 8:31
66   Isaiah 53:7

looked the man straight in the eye and asked, 'About whom, I ask you, does the prophet say this—about himself or about someone else?'"[67]

"What did he say?" Gamal asked.

"He told me that this was referring to the one the Hebrews call Messiah, but which Isaiah was describing as the Suffering Servant." Negasi paused, then said, "I know something about being a servant. That's all I've ever been. But the things he explained to me set before me Someone unlike anyone I've ever known—or even heard of, for that matter."

"How so?" asked Gamal.

"Well," Negasi said, pausing thoughtfully for a moment, "this servant served not merely a master or his household, not even a great monarch like Queen Candace." His voice trailed off as his mind wandered.

Now he gets quiet! thought Gamal. Dangling the question in an attempt to retrieve Negasi to the moment, he asked, "Whom did this Suffering Servant . . . *serve?*"

"God," was all Negasi could say but then switched his answer abruptly to an urgent "Us! I mean, He served God by serving us." But the words still didn't convey what the big Ethiopian was trying to say, and a puzzled look swept over his face.

"I don't think I understand," Gamal admitted.

"I didn't either," said Negasi. "But he continued speaking to me of Him, referring to many other places in the Hebrew Scriptures. I learned that all these prophesies had been fulfilled in a Man who had been killed not long ago."

The big man gathered himself, as if it would take all his strength and then some to explain it. "This Man was more than just a man.

---

67   Acts 8:34

He was God as well. God and man. Both. Completely." He paused. "I'm sorry. I'm still trying to work it all out in my mind, and I'm not explaining nearly as well as this man did."

"It's okay," Gamal assured him. "Please continue."

"He said He was their King, and that didn't go over well with the Romans. This Man-Who-was-God fulfilled all that the Hebrew Scriptures required, both the Law and the Prophets, and then, as the passage in Isaiah predicted, suffered and died in our place as an offering for sin. He, Who had no sin, died bearing the sin-debt of all His people, laid upon Him by God, His Father. All that, so His people could be free of their sin-debt and of its power over them."

"That's remarkable," Gamal admitted.

"Oh, it gets better, believe me," Negasi said.

Gamal leaned in to catch every word.

"They told me this Man, Who had died, came back to life."

"What?!" Gamal shot back incredulously.

"I know, I know," admitted Negasi. "I had a hard time believing it, too. But the man swore that there were scores of witnesses. Not only the Messiah's closest friends, but as many as five hundred saw Him alive at one appearing."

Gamal must have looked skeptical because Negasi shot him a look that said, *Don't jump ship quite yet.* The big man motioned with his hands for Gamal to give him just a little more time. So, Gamal asked, "Where is this Man now?"

"He ascended into the heavens right before the eyes of His followers."

Now both sat silently, as they considered the possibilities of it all.

Finally Gamal asked, "What do you make of it?"

"Well, I have to tell you, my friend . . . I know it sounds a bit far-fetched, but something within me seemed to cry 'Yes!' to everything I heard. It was all written beforehand, and there are eyewitnesses galore. And my heart is witnessing to me that it is all true."

After a moment of reflection, he continued, "This may seem strange, but it was as if in those moments, I not only learned all these amazing things about the Jewish Messiah, but I also learned something about myself that I'd never known before."

"Like what?"

"That I had been looking for a King. The thought had never occurred to me. But I suddenly realized, there was a throne room within me that had been yearning for a Ruler—the perfect, benevolent Ruler."

Negasi continued after a brief pause: "I've been at the highest levels of my government. I serve a queen, for goodness' sake! But I'd never realized I was ruling my own life—and not doing a very good job of it. In that moment—I don't know how to explain it—there was a yearning within me—an irrepressible cry almost—that kept wanting to address this Man-Who-is-God and to designate Him *my* King. My name, Negasi, means 'He will wear a crown,' but I now realized it wasn't a crown I needed but Someone to sit on the throne of my life."

Gamal didn't know even how to ask his new friend to go on, but he desperately wanted him to. As Negasi described his own inner struggle, Gamal heard an echo of his own. To his relief, Negasi continued, "So, I told the man who had joined me in the chariot how I was feeling. He smiled a knowing smile and said he knew just what I was talking about. Just then, out in the middle of the desert, we came upon a small oasis. The cattle needed a drink, as did we. But more than anything else, I told the man I wanted this King to rule my life. He told me the Man-Who-is-God called those who would follow Him to be washed in water as a public expression of their desire to be made clean and new by Him."

"And?" Gamal grabbed again at the now-familiar verbal prod.

"We got out of the chariot. We walked down into the oasis. The man plunged me beneath the water and brought me back up, declaring me to be a subject of King Jesus. Then, just as he had come, the man suddenly disappeared. He was just gone!"

Gamal's mind reeled; the room seemed to spin; and he reached his hand back to the bench as if to hold himself steady. "What did you say?"

"He disappeared."

"No! No, before that," Gamal insisted.

"He declared me to be a subject of King Jesus," Negasi said. "And so I am—a servant of Queen Candace by occupation; a subject of King Jesus by devotion."

"Jesus," Gamal verbally muttered under his breath. His eyes seemed to search for a focal point far beyond the familiar world of his woodshop. As if transported to another time, he continued to softly repeat to himself the name, "Jesus." Then, "No. Couldn't be. There's no way!"

Now Negasi was the one lost. "What are you saying, my friend? What are you thinking?"

"Did you say His name is Jesus?" Gamal asked insistently.

"Yes, His name is Jesus. They call him the Christ." Negasi studied his friend's face and plied him, "Why do you ask, Gamal?"

But Gamal was far away and unable to be summoned. Was that hope upon his face? Or terror? Negasi could not quite make it out.

Again, he begged, "Why do you ask, my friend?"

The table project would have to wait. Gamal finally drifted back to the moment and locked eyes with his Ethiopian customer, now a friend-turned-witness. "Can *I* now tell *you* a story?"

Negasi's eyes widened like saucers as he nodded his head, anxious to hear how his experience might find an echo in this man's life. At this point, Negasi had come to expect the unexpected.

"It was decades ago, thirty years or more," Gamal began. "I was perhaps fifteen at the time. I was apprenticing under my father, who was a fine Egyptian woodworker. You know that we Egyptians were perfecting woodworking when others were still pulling up rocks to sit on?"

Negasi shot him a look that said, *I'm not here for a history lesson about Egyptian woodworking!*

"Sorry," Gamal mumbled. Clearing his throat, he continued in a stronger voice, "I was apprenticing under my father. I happened through the market one day, and I noticed a small display of simple furniture. I paused to study them. They were plain. Nothing fancy. None of the intricate inlay of my father's work. But then I began to study the joints. I'd never seen anything quite like them. Then I sat on a chair. Steady as a stone!"

Negasi cleared his throat and raised an eyebrow.

Gamal again mumbled, "Sorry. But it is a part of the story."

"Okay, continue *please!*"

"So, I was quite taken with the quality of work. As I lay on the ground studying the underside of a chair and table, the carpenter approached. A bit embarrassed, I jumped up, dusting myself off. I stammered and said lamely, 'I've never seen anything quite like these before.'

"He asked in reply, 'Are you a student of carpentry?' To which I responded by explaining my apprenticeship. The man demurred a bit as I raved about his work. 'Oh, it is just simple stuff; nothing as fancy as what you Egyptians turn out.' But I told him it was the joints that were a thing of beauty. I'd never seen anything so perfectly joined, so tight, so solid."

Gamal got lost in the memory for a moment and then snapped back with an apologetic look. "I'm not usually so forward, but next thing I knew, I was asking him if he would teach me joinery. I had to admit that I couldn't pay him but if I could just come watch him, ask a few questions, study his technique, see his tools—"

Negasi interrupted, "I'm sorry, my friend, but I'm not seeing the connection. How does this have anything to do with me coming under Jesus' rule?"

"I'm getting to that," Gamal assured him. "I studied under him each day after I completed things with my father. I learned some great technical skills. But the point is that one day as we were working, I stopped asking him about his occupation and turned to more personal inquiries. The story he told me has remained with me all these decades, dancing on the periphery of my thoughts and always begging for some resolution in my life. But I've yet to come to that resolve." He paused, then added, "Until, perhaps, today."

The big Ethiopian handed Gamal his glass of water, urging him to take a deep draught and then to continue.

"I learned that his name was Joseph. He was a Hebrew, from Judea. His wife's name was Mary, and they had a baby boy."

"Let me guess," said Negasi. "The Baby's name was Jesus?"

"Yes! Yes, it was . . . *is* . . . um, I'm not sure now what word to use. You've confused me."

"Are you thinking this Baby Jesus is my King Jesus?" Negasi asked incredulously.

"Well, I don't know," Gamal replied. "That's what's got me wondering."

"Why? Why would you think this might be so?"

"It's the story that Joseph told me."

"Then, by all means, proceed!" the Ethiopian urged.

"Well, you see, Joseph and Mary hadn't been . . . exactly . . . married."

Negasi's eyebrows raised again.

Gamal continued, "They were betrothed. Committed, but not living together as husband and wife just yet. So when Mary told Joseph she was pregnant, you can understand his confusion. She told him that an angel appeared to her and told her that she would bear the Son of God and that He would be the long-awaited King of Israel. She told Joseph she had protested because of her virginity, but the angel simply said God's Holy Spirit would take care of it."

Gamal paused to let his friend's mind catch up, and when he thought it wise, he continued. "So, you can imagine the quandary in which Joseph found himself. What would their families think? What would their community think? What did *he* think? He had made a commitment to her; he wanted to believe her . . . But, honestly . . ."

Gamal and Negasi both imagined the rending emotions. Then Gamal said, "He told me he didn't know quite what to do until an angel appeared to him and confirmed the story, just as Mary had described it. And Joseph was told to name the Baby Jesus because 'He would save His people from their sins.'"[68]

---

68   Matthew 1:21

"When he reported this to Mary, she told him that the angel had also told her they must name the baby Jesus. So, sensing together that God was in this, they moved forward, difficult as it was. While Mary was heavy with child, Caesar Augustus ordered a census of the entire empire. The Hebrews don't do it like most of the rest of us—they demanded to return to their ancestral homes and register there. So, Joseph and a very-pregnant Mary traveled south to a village called Bethlehem, as I recall. While there, Mary gave birth to Jesus."

"But how did they end up here in On, Egypt?" Negasi asked.

"Well, the story gets even more complicated. The family had stayed in Bethlehem for some time to let the Baby and Mary grow stronger. Then one night, an angel warned Joseph in a dream that the local Roman ruler was going to murder his Son and that they must flee to Egypt immediately. So, they did."

"And?"

"And they arrived here in On and settled in. Joseph did his best to provide by making tables and chairs. That's when I met him. That's when I learned their story. I looked upon his Baby Boy and wondered about the things predicted about Him. How could all this be wrapped up in a tiny infant?

"They eventually returned to Israel. That was the last news I had on them, until today."

Now both men settled into silence. Could the Jesus each one knew really be the same Person? After some time in thought, Gamal and Negasi clasped hands and locked eyes, knowing they were knit together in a drama too vast for either of them to fully comprehend. They also knew that they must keep searching until they found the answers for which they longed.

The next morning, Gamal was back in his woodshop, surrounded again by the familiar sights, sounds, and smells that made this his sanctuary. He willed himself to concentrate, applying himself to the table project. He wondered about the fresh passion that swept over him to make *this* table the best he'd ever produced. He worked the bow lathe, turning out the legs. He smoothed the tabletop with his plane. The rich beauty began to emerge as Gamal's skillful hands performed their magic.

Late in the afternoon, Negasi appeared again at his door. He barely noticed the prized table that had brought them together. There was an urgent message to deliver. "Gamal, my friend, you won't believe this! I have located a small band of Jesus-followers here in On."

"Here?" a stunned Gamal stammered.

"Yes, just a handful, but they, too, like me, have submitted their lives to Him. They have invited us to their next meeting, wishing to hear our stories and to share their own with us."

"When is this to take place?" Gamal inquired.

"Tomorrow night."

Gamal nodded his head thoughtfully. As Negasi came inside and settled on the bench, Gamal went back to work on the table. Silence enveloped them for some time, both lost in thought. Each wondered at the closeness he felt with the other man he'd known for only two days. So quickly yet so deeply, they had become fellow travelers on a quest that reached beyond this world but had formed a crossroads in their experience.

Negasi suddenly rose, and he began to run his hands slowly over the now fully-turned table legs. He clearly admired the craftsmanship that rendered them so symmetrically perfect, identical in every way. He glanced at Gamal, who had turned from planing the tabletop to creating a mortise by which one of the legs would be joined to the tabletop.

"What is that you are doing?" inquired the enormous Ethiopian. Chips flew about the shop as Gamal deftly applied hammer to chisel, carving out a hole in one corner of the otherwise pristine upper portion of the table. "Why are you marring this lovely piece of wood with that hole?"

"This is not just a hole," Gamal replied without looking up from his work. "This is called a mortise."

"A what-ise?" Negasi asked with a bewildered look upon his face.

"A mortise. I am creating this so that I can then fashion a tenon on the top of each leg. The tenon will be fitted precisely and perfectly to the mortise. This is what makes for that rock-solid stability you so admired in the table you saw at the home of Amosis."

The court official nodded knowingly and sat again to watch and learn as Gamal went about his work.

Sometime during his labors, Gamal spoke again: "*This* is what I learned from Joseph. His creations were simple, at least by Egyptian standards. But his joinery was like no other."

A bit later, he continued, "My father was at first aghast that I was taking lessons from a Hebrew carpenter. He recounted to me many times the glories of Egyptian woodworking. Did I not know that Egyptians had been working wood long before the Hebrews? My father refused to even meet Joseph. But eventually, when he began to see the results in my work, he quietly offered his admiration. I took it as a signal he approved."

By the end of the day, the basic structure was complete. Both men stood back and took in the sight. Negasi laid his big hand on the table to check its stability. *Perfect!*

The next day, Gamal worked alone, creating the intricate inlays for the tabletop. As he was finishing his evening meal with Rania, Nour, and Nubia, a rap came at the door. Gamal opened the door to the sight of the towering Ethiopian, whose dress clearly showed that he was a man of dignity and position. Rania's eyes immediately fell to the floor in deference, but Nour and Nubia's eyes grew wide at the sight of the immense man as he and their father embraced in welcome.

Gamal introduced everyone and announced that he would be occupied away from home for the evening. He thanked Rania for the fine meal and kissed the children goodnight, promising to check on them when he returned.

With that, the men were gone into the labyrinth of narrow streets. Though this was Gamal's city, it was Negasi who led the way. Finally, as they rounded another corner, Negasi announced, "This is it," motioning toward a nondescript home.

To Gamal, it didn't look different than any other home in town. But the owner welcomed him at the door like a long-lost brother. Negasi, with the studied practice of years of court formalities, introduced Gamal to his newest friend. Instantly, he was pulled inside and paraded before the seven others who filled the room. Again, there were hearty welcomes and glad embraces, then an invitation to be seated.

When everyone settled in, the homeowner turned to his spiritual brothers and sisters, announcing, "As I told you, tonight, we are privileged to welcome two guests. Negasi is the man I told you all about. Oh, what a tale he has to share with us tonight! And this is his friend, Gamal, who is exploring what all this means. I hear he, too, has a remarkable story to tell."

With that, Negasi launched into the story of his official visit to Jerusalem, his exposure to the Hebrew Scriptures, his questions, the sudden appearance of the witness, his heart-change at the news about Jesus, his subsequent baptism, and how the man disappeared as quickly as he had appeared.

Everyone sat in riveted attention, drinking in every word. Smiles danced across their faces. Heads bobbed up and down not only in acknowledgement that they were following the story but also in praise of the Author of it all. Negasi leaned back, signaling that he had finished his tale and would rest his voice. Spontaneously, hands came together in claps of wonder and worship as hearts rejoiced.

All eyes then turned to Gamal. He felt his face flush. *What am I doing here?* He wanted desperately to burst out of the door and be gone. But something held him in place. He awkwardly cleared his throat and attempted a beginning. He paused, clearly uncomfortable. He stammered a couple of incoherent sounds then stopped again.

"Please, Gamal," the homeowner said. "You are among friends!"

It was true. The faces all welcomed him. Before he quite knew what he was doing, he told them of his long-ago relationship with a man named Joseph, of his wife Mary and her miraculous pregnancy, the Baby they'd named Jesus at the behest of an angel, and their angelic warning to flee for their lives to Egypt.

Everyone was clearly just as pleased to hear Gamal's story, but it evoked more of a contemplative silence. They had heard that Jesus briefly spent time in Egypt, and they had wondered about the details, but this was the first eyewitness account they had heard.

The holy hush gave way to a question. "And are you, too, a follower of Jesus?"

All eyes fixed on Gamal as they anticipated his answer. Again, the burning fever rose in his cheeks. He was unsure how to answer and uncomfortable in the spotlight. He spent his days working alone. Now, at the center of attention, he felt out of his element.

All he was able to offer in reply was a simple, "I am not certain." His eyes fell to the floor; his shoulders slumped; and he exhaled deeply.

"What would make you certain?" one of the men asked. "I mean, about Jesus."

Gamal was quiet as he thought about the question. After some moments, he said, "I do have questions."

"Such as?"

"Well," the carpenter said, wavering just a bit as if he had never actually articulated them beyond the space in his own head. "Well, I understand from what I have heard from Negasi that Jesus was both God and man and that He died to bear away the consequences of all our sin. I know that many have testified to His being alive from the dead and going back to His Father in Heaven."

He paused.

"Yes," the group spontaneously replied in unison, urging him to continue.

"But how can these things be? I mean, *can* they be?"

The homeowner said, "Perhaps it would help if I tell you the experience several of us had."

Gamal was grateful to surrender the floor.

The man launched in. "We—several of us—traveled to Jerusalem. It was a high day for their people, a time they call Pentecost. We had all been in one way or another exposed to Jewish religious claims here in Egypt and had begun attending a study of their Scriptures. We were seekers, I guess you'd say. The city was jammed with people from all over the world. If we'd been mere tourists, we would have picked another time to travel, but we weren't there for sightseeing."

"Oh?" Gamal queried, trying to appear nonchalant.

"Yes, we'd grown interested and wanted to know more. But now we've come to see that God was shaping all of this, from beginning to end. We were milling about the crowds when we began to hear a commotion. A group of men were making a ruckus. At first, we thought they'd tipped their wineskins a little early in the day. But as we listened more intently, we heard a remarkable thing. Even now, it defies full understanding."

"What was it?" Gamal inquired, growing enthralled.

"We heard these men speaking in our language—Egyptian. But there were people around us from all over the world, and they were turning to the others in their travel parties and wondering how they were hearing the men speak in *their* own language. There were Parthians and Medes and Elamites and residents of Mesopotamia. There were others from Libya and Rome. There were Cretans and Arabians. And all of them were hearing the men speak in their own language, even while we continued to hear them speak to us in Egyptian. It was . . . well . . . astounding!"

"But what were they saying?" Gamal now begged.

"They were describing for us amazing things that God had done. When they had the massive crowd's attention, one of them, a man named Peter, stood up and told us of Jesus. He outlined from their Scriptures how Jesus was the fulfillment of all their hopes, all *our* hopes. We all, as if one, asked, 'What shall we do?'[69] He told us to turn from our ways, turn to God through Jesus, and be baptized."

"Just like me!" Negasi jumped in enthusiastically.

Gamal looked at his friend, nodded, then started to object. "But . . ."

One of the men raised his voice. "One of the Hebrew prophets asked, 'Can the Ethiopian change his skin or the leopard his spots?'[70] Negasi, your skin remains as it always has, but by your own confession, you are a new man."

"Yes, it is true," the big Ethiopian admitted with his toothy smile.

The man then turned back to Gamal, "Would you like to be made new, too?"

Again, Gamal felt a flash of heat surge, this time through his entire body. *How did I get myself into this? Why am I here?* he wondered to himself.

"But, but . . ." Gamal stammered. "I am not a Jew! For that matter, neither are you! How can any of this be true for *me*, for *us*?"

One of the men responded for them all. "You told us of Joseph. We believe your testimony. It fits with the general account we've learned about the holy family's early days. But the Bible tells of another, earlier Joseph. He was a son of Israel himself. God providentially arranged for that Joseph to be brought into Egypt as a slave. There, God put His favor upon him, and he rose from a prison cell to be the second highest ruler of our land."

"Yes," Gamal nodded. "I remember something about that from my history lessons."

---

69   Acts 2:37
70   Jeremiah 13:23

"Did you know," the man continued, "that Pharaoh gave Joseph a wife from right here in On? One of the high priest's own daughters."

"Really?" Gamal replied, clearly astonished.

"Absolutely! That means that two of Israel's tribes began with fifty percent Egyptian blood in them!"

Gamal pulled his head back as he considered the idea.

"It is true," the man continued, "that we Egyptians have not always been good to the Hebrews, but I want to read to you a passage we discovered in one of their prophets when we were in Jerusalem."

With that, he reached back and pulled out a large scroll. "This is from the prophet Isaiah," he said. "The same one you were reading, Negasi."

The Ethiopian's head bobbed up and down, accompanied again by his infectious, wide smile.

The man read, "'In that day there will be five cities in the land of Egypt that speak the language of Canaan and swear allegiance to the Lord of hosts.'"[71]

Gamal was puzzled, and thought, *He spoke* our *language so we could speak* His?

But the man went on without interruption. "'One of these will be called the City of Destruction.'"

Here, he paused a moment to explain. "In Hebrew, the word for 'destruction' rhymes with their word for 'sun.' We're told that the prophet was probably making a play on words, referring to 'the city of the sun.'"

The man paused now to let the thought sink in. Gamal raised his eyes as if he was pleading, *This can't be!*

---

71   Isaiah 19:18

"Oh, yes," the man said. "He is speaking of our very city, On, the city of the sun."

"But why call it 'the City of Destruction'?" Gamal asked.

"Isn't that what we deserve?" the man asked. "And isn't that what we've all been observing over the past several decades? With the rise of Alexandria, all our glory has shifted. People are leaving. The Romans are dismantling our famed obelisks and taking them elsewhere in their empire. You have to admit we're slowly coming to nothing."

Again, he paused to let the assessment sink in.

He launched back into the scroll. "The prophet went on, 'In that day there will be an altar to the Lord in the midst of the land of Egypt, and a pillar to the Lord at its border.'"[72]

He paused for effect, then said, "Did you hear that? Not pillars to Ra and Atum here in On, but a pillar to the Lord at the border!"

He continued reading. "'It will be a sign and a witness to the Lord of hosts in the land of Egypt. When they cry to the Lord because of oppressors, he will send them a savior and defender, and deliver them. And the Lord will make himself known to the Egyptians, and the Egyptians will know the Lord in that day and worship with sacrifice and offering, and they will make vows to the Lord and perform them.'"[73]

"Did you hear that?" the man asked again. "God sent us a Savior! Not just to the Hebrews, but to *us*! He promised to make Himself known to *us*. What do you think our story, *your* story, means, if not that He is keeping His Word to us?"

Gamal was deep in thought now.

---

72   Isaiah 19:19
73   Isaiah 19:20-21

"And the prophet went on to promise, 'He will listen to their pleas for mercy and heal them' and that He will so bless those Egyptians who do call upon Him that He will call them—are you ready for this?—'Egypt my people.'"[74]

Silence enveloped everyone in the room. Gamal turned the phrase over in his mind, not realizing he was also verbalizing it softly. "'Egypt my people.'"

The hush was shattered when Gamal suddenly jumped to his feet and headed for the door. He fumbled out a hasty word of thanks for their hospitality and apologetically said, "I have to think!" With that, he was gone from the house.

Negasi looked to the host and the other gathered guests and said, "Perhaps we should pray for our friend."

That they did, earnestly, well into the night.

The next morning, Gamal was back in his woodshop, a bit wearier than usual because of his sleepless night. But he needed the familiar surroundings of his shop. He was putting the finishing touches on the top of Negasi's table when a knock came at the door. There his large friend stood with a gleaming, bright smile.

"A glorious morning, don't you think?" he announced, a bit too cheerfully for Gamal.

"Yes, it is," Gamal replied with significantly less enthusiasm.

Negasi stepped past Gamal, welcomed himself inside, and took his spot on the bench. Then he saw his table. He rose in admiration. He gazed adoringly at it, first reaching out a hand to touch it and then

---

74   Isaiah 19:22-25

withdrawing his hand as if he might defile this object of beauty. His hand went over his mouth instead, and he turned a wonder-filled expression upon Gamal. "It is . . . beautiful!" He paused reverently and then added, "My queen will be most grateful. Thank you, my friend! You'd best be prepared for orders to pour in from Ethiopia."

But Gamal slumped upon the bench, his face downcast. He fumbled with the rag he had been using to buff the table to a high sheen.

Negasi came close and folded his massive frame, settling on his knees before his troubled friend.

"Talk to me, my friend. Tell me what is in your heart."

Gamal fumbled further with the rag. Finally he said, "It feels like a hole."

"What feels like a hole?" Negasi asked.

"My heart. It feels like there is a hole in my heart. I have been aware of it for many years. I have been waiting, seeking, longing for that which would fill it. But now, at this news of Jesus, I am afraid that if I ask him to do so, I may be disappointed."

"Oh, my friend! You will not be disappointed. Jesus could never disappoint."

"I thought you'd say that," Gamal reluctantly replied.

With that, Negasi rose up to his full height, taking an especially dignified stance. Gamal lifted his eyes to see what he was up to.

Negasi then drew upon his deepest, richest tones as he said with the formality of a royal introduction, "I am Negasi, from the court of Candace, Queen of Ethiopia! It is my professional duty to make introductions. I am here, Gamal, to introduce you to my King."

Gamal wrinkled his forehead.

Negasi relaxed slightly, his tone softening into a friendly pleading. "Gamal, my friend. I am courtier of a leading foreign monarch. Jesus came to me as a King and asked to sit upon the throne of my heart. Our friends are Egyptian *seekers*—He spoke to them in their own tongue to call them to be found in Him." Negasi paused for effect and then said, "You are a carpenter. A fine one, as this table testifies. To you, Jesus has come as a Carpenter."

An even more puzzled expression crossed Gamal's face.

Undaunted, Negasi continued, "Has it ever occurred to you that your encounter with Jesus' father Joseph was no accident?"

"What do you mean?"

"I mean, you told me just yesterday that you prepare the—what did you call it? mortise—to receive the tenon. The hole is perfectly fit to receive the tenon. This is what makes for a solid, stable table, yes?"

"Yes," replied the carpenter, surprised the courtier had been thinking so deeply about his profession.

"Has it occurred to you that God sent His Son and His earthly family to you all those years ago to begin preparing the mortise of your heart, that you might this day receive Jesus as the One for Whom your heart has been perfectly readied?"

Gamal took in the thought.

Negasi was on a roll, so he continued. "Has it ever occurred to you that God gave you this skill with wood so He might call you to Himself?

"And one more thing," Negasi said.

"What's that?" Gamal asked.

"If Joseph was a carpenter, what did that make Jesus?"

"Excuse me?" Gamal asked.

"What did Jesus do with Himself prior to age thirty when He began His ministry?"

"I don't know. How would I know?"

Incredulously, Negasi asked, "What do sons of carpenters become?"

Gamal's expression gave away that still he was not tracking.

"What did *your* father do?"

"He was a carpenter!"

"What do *you* do?"

"Just what my father trained me to do; with a little supplement from Joseph."

Now the big Ethiopian pressed his last and best point. "Do you not know that Jesus, too, was a carpenter?"

A look of wonder swept over Gamal's face, as if the sun had just risen to shine through the window of his soul, exposing the void within for what it truly was.

Gamal gazed up at Negasi and said, "God's Son came to me, a carpenter, as a carpenter . . . having perfectly fitted the hole in my heart to receive him! All these years I have been custom-made to meet Him!"

Hearing Gamal's confession of realization and faith, a wide smile spread across Negasi's face. He stretched out his arms to receive his new brother in the Lord.

The next morning, Gamal was back in his woodshop early. He drank in the familiar smells and the street noises. He took in the glint of the sun's first full rays pouring through the window. He studied the dust dancing in the sunshine. It was all so familiar, but it was also new—the colors more brilliant, the smells richer, the sun brighter.

This morning, instead of rising to his work, Gamal first sank to his knees in the sawdust. As he bowed to pray, he repeated to himself a line he'd heard his new brothers read from one of the Hebrew prophets. "'For you who fear my name, the sun of righteousness shall rise with healing in its wings.'"[75]

Prayerfully, Gamal drank in the sunshine and thought to himself, *The light pouring through my window isn't half bad either.*

As the years passed, Gamal found his heart more and more fitted to the inward presence of Jesus. Progressively, his life grew strong, solid, sure, steady. Increasingly the Jewish Carpenter from Nazareth completed His custom work in the Egyptian carpenter from On.

75   Malachi 4:2

ADVENT ARMIES

HEAVEN BUZZED WITH A FLURRY of activity. The resulting tumult was unmatched by anything the angelic hosts had ever experienced. Not even the creation of the universe had been this exciting. Sure, they had sung in united joy as, at the command of God, light split darkness, earth separated from water, and lifeforms popped into existence. The sudden animation of the first human by God's own breath had taken away theirs momentarily before they rose in one united round of deafening applause.

But this was different; it was somehow bigger, deeper, and even more fundamental. The angelic host were up to their wings in final preparations for the promised re-creation—the restoration of all that had been stolen from the universe. Even the thunderous victory-shout they let loose when Jesus rose from the dead would prove to have been a dress rehearsal for what was about to transpire. That thunderous roar of triumph had shaken the foundations of hell itself. What was afoot now would shatter them forever and bring it all down around the devil's ears.

The glimmer in every angel's eye was more glorious than ever. They were beside themselves in anticipation.

But there were final preparations to make. And they were in earnest to see them through. Everything had to be just right for Jesus' second advent.

They awaited a few ministering spirits sent out on final errands on earth, fitting out the details of history in preparation for the unveiling of Jesus in His glory. Each polished and prepped and made ready for their part in the grandest display of force the creation had ever seen.

Michael cleared his throat in a way that made myriads upon myriads of humanly innumerable angels instantly lift their heads from their work and cast a responsive glance his way. He didn't have to raise his voice to command their wills. He said simply, "All right, let's bring it in. Circle up."

And that they did. In a perfect display of ordered precision, the angels each found their place in what would have seemed but half a second on earth. In every direction and as far as a human eye would have been able to see, there stood at attention the gleaming, shining warriors who had spent their entire existence either in the presence of their Commander or actively carrying out His will.

Michael paused to take in the sight. Never had Heaven dispatched the entire angelic force on a single mission. But this would be unlike anything that had ever happened before; and it would be the defining point for everything that would follow. The archangel, as Michael's rank designated him, spotted not one flaw, not one item out of place as the armies of Heaven stood for review.

He broke the hushed silence. "I don't need to tell you that we are on the cusp of everything we've ever desired. I know you have made ready. Thank you for your service and devotion to our Master. As we await His imminent command, allow me to have a few from our number share about their role in Jesus' first advent."

A hush of anticipation swept through the ranks as heads turned and angels gazed into one another's eyes and nodded their heads in expectancy. They never tired of hearing this story.

Michael glanced toward one angel and nodded. "Gabriel, will you start us off by sharing what it was like as you served to prepare the way for Jesus' first coming?"

The powerful angel moved forward, and as he did, his luminescence grew until any non-heavenly being would have had to shield their eyes, lest they be blinded forever. "As you know, our King's first arrival was no simple affair. It was a complex arrangement of a multitude of decisions, choices, thoughts, and actions by a vast array of players. Our Master's wisdom, as we all know, once again proved brilliant. My role was to prepare the way for the preparer-of-the-way for His arrival upon Earth. Long before—in earth years, at least—the Spirit had spoken of this forerunner through the prophets Isaiah and Malachi. It was my privilege to aid in putting the reality into motion. I was directed to a faithful priest by the name of Zechariah. Though blameless and righteous in their adherence to the Master's word and advanced in years, he and his wife were barren. By the Master's arrangement, the lot fell to Zechariah to serve in the temple. So, when he entered alone into the inner chambers to appear in the Lord's presence, I manifested myself at the right side of the altar of incense."

With a downward glance and a brief pause, Gabriel continued, "I'm sorry to say that I nearly did the old fellow in."

A low chuckle arose from a few in the front row.

"I quickly said, 'Do not be afraid. Your prayer has been heard, and your wife Elizabeth will bear you a son. You shall call his name John.

You will have joy and gladness, and many will rejoice at his birth.' He looked a bit stunned, and I wasn't sure how much was getting through, but I continued, 'Your son will go before the Lord in the spirit and power of Elijah, to make ready for the Lord a people prepared.'"[76]

Gabriel paused again. He wrung at the white raiment of his robes for a moment and then with a pained expression added, "I wish he hadn't done it, but he questioned how he would know this would happen."

A disapproving murmur arose from those nearest the reporting angel. He continued, "So I had to give him a sign. I said, 'You will be silent and unable to speak until the day that these things take place, because you did not believe my words, which will be fulfilled in their time.'[77] After that, I withdrew, and he exited the inner chambers of the temple. When the people saw him, they realized that though his lips moved, no sound came out, and they observed the color drained from his face. They rightly concluded that something supernatural had happened within the temple chambers."

Gabriel lifted his head and with a steady voice reported, "Everything unfolded, by the Master's doing, just as I had been instructed to announce. Zechariah's wife, Elizabeth, was with child."

A murmur again swept over the angelic hosts, this time a reverent one. Michael lifted his hand, and the sound died away. He then turned back to the reporting angel, saying, "Please continue, for we all know this was not the full extent of your role."

The shining one nodded his head in agreement and said, "Yes, this is true. The honor bestowed me is beyond words. When Elizabeth was two-thirds of the way through her pregnancy, I was sent again,

---

76   Luke 1:13-17
77   Luke 1:20

this time not to an aged, barren woman, but to the faithful, young woman—almost a child, really. And this time, I went not to the temple in Jerusalem but to the village of Nazareth, where she lived with her family."

Michael interrupted, asking, "This assignment was similar to your first but was profoundly different in a number of ways, yes?"

Gabriel nodded his agreement. "Yes, absolutely. It was the same in that I was announcing a conception, gestation, and birth. But the players were profoundly different and the earthly implications far more complicated."

With a reflective look upon his face, he continued, "The asset was actually a young relative of Elizabeth, but she was as yet a virgin. She had been betrothed to a fine man named Joseph, but they had not yet come together as husband and wife. How does one tell such an innocent one that she will be pregnant, blamelessly so in the eyes of God? And of course, the child she would carry, birth, and raise would be infinitely more glorious."

"Tell us about it," Michael invited with a nod.

"Well, having seen what my presence and words did to old Zechariah, I was nervous about my approach to the young woman, Mary. So I started out as positively as I thought possible: 'Greetings, O favored one, the Lord is with you!'"[78] He paused with a slightly pained expression and then continued, "But I'm afraid there's only so much finessing one of us can do in such circumstances. I scared her quite badly. So I said, 'Do not be afraid, Mary, for you have found favor with God.'[79] And then I figured I might as well forge ahead. So,

---

78   Luke 1:28
79   Luke 1:30

I continued, 'Behold, you will conceive in your womb and bear a son, and you shall call his name Jesus. He will be great and will be called the Son of the Most High. And the Lord God will give to him the throne of his father David, and he will reign over the house of Jacob forever, and of his kingdom there will be no end.'"[80]

Gabriel winced just a bit at the memory. He recalled how he'd felt he had perhaps over-spoken in the moment.

"And her response?" asked Michael.

"You can imagine her confusion. She, of course, asked about how this would be since she had never been with a man."

"And your answer?" Michael asked again.

Gabriel chuckled a bit under his breath. "Well," he said and then paused, "how do you explain the unexplainable? I told her the Holy Spirit would take care of it."

At that, every angel in creation whispered in unison "Amen!" All of Heaven fell silent for a moment at the very thought.

Michael, wanting to move the report along, nudged, "And?"

"*And* I told her about her relative Elizabeth. I finished by reminding her, 'Nothing will be impossible with God.'"[81]

Another "Amen!" arose from the gathered host, this one a bit more emphatic and militaristic.

"And her response?" Michael asked.

Gabriel put his hand to his mouth as if to gather his composure. If angels weep, it certainly looked like he might. Finally, in a voice filled with emotion, he announced, "She said, 'Behold, I am the servant of the Lord; let it be to me according to your word.'"[82]

---

80   Luke 1:31-33
81   Luke 1:37
82   Luke 1:38

This time, there was an excited flutter of the wings from every ministering spirit who understood innately the sentiments of the chosen woman, though they marveled at its rarity among the human race.

"Thank you, Gabe," Michael said with a hand laid appreciatively upon the angel's back. Gabriel nodded and receded again into the ranks of the assembled armies of God.

Michael then stated the obvious. "As you could well guess and already know, this created some loose ends on earth that the Master asked us to tend to." With that, he signaled with his eye for another angel to step to the fore.

As he did, his countenance, much like Gabriel's, grew brighter and seemed to emit something of the glory of the One He serves.

"Brother, will you share with us your part in this unfolding drama of our King's first advent?"

"Certainly," the angel said with a deferential bow of his head to the archangel.

He cleared his throat and said, "We can all imagine the complications that Gabriel's announcement to young Mary created. Of first priority was the man to whom she was betrothed. So, I, too, visited Nazareth. Joseph had been weighing every option available to him. He, being a righteous man, had decided to simply divorce her quietly and go his way. The family angst, the social pressure, and the spiritual confusion was real. He was doing the best he knew to do, humanly. But it was my responsibility to convince him to choose the way of faith. No easy task with news like he had received."

"So how did you pull it off?" Michael asked on behalf of every other listening angel.

"I just quietly slipped myself into one of his dreams," the angel reported. "I decided to be direct, telling him, 'Joseph, son of David, do not fear to take Mary as your wife, for that which is conceived in her is from the Holy Spirit.'"[83]

Now it was Michael who seemed bemused, with the corners of his lips turning slightly upward at the thought. "And then?" he asked.

"And then I said, 'She will bear a son, and you shall call his name Jesus, for he will save his people from their sins.'"[84]

At the very thought of it, the angels gasped, as if they'd never heard the news before. The thought of the Master dying still overburdened their mental circuits. But the thought of this kind of love for such as the human race was even more stunning to the angelic host.

"Did it work?" Michael asked, though they all knew the answer.

"Yes," the angel reported. "I dropped a memory into his mind—a recollection of what Isaiah the prophet had said about the virgin conceiving and the resulting child being Immanuel—God with them."

"Ah," Michael said, nodding in agreement with the rest of the gathered angels. "Nothing like God's own word to ignite faith!"

Then, as the reporting angel slipped back into line, the archangel took up the narrative on his own. "We all know that the pregnancy of Elizabeth continued, despite her advanced age, in a healthy way and culminated in the birth of a vigorous man-child. Though there was confusion at her instance of naming the child John, Zechariah was given his voice in the nick of time and, faithful to our brother's instructions, affirmed this was to be his son's name."

---

83   Matthew 1:20
84   Matthew 1:21; Luke 1:31

"We know, too, that Joseph faithfully stayed with Mary. Her pregnancy also was healthy, though the Master's providence again worked to make a dizzying array of details come together so the Child would be born, as previously announced through the prophets, in Bethlehem."

"And who can forget *that* night! As difficult as it had been for us to see our Master so humbled as to take up residence as a gestating child in a human mother's womb, none of us was ready for the sight of His actual birth and to behold Him not only in human form but as fully *human*, and what's more, a fully human *infant*."

Again angels covered their mouths to stifle the mummer over the amazing grace they struggled to understand.

"Difficult as it is for us to comprehend such love, we knew despite its humblest of earthly circumstances, it deserved a heavenly round of applause. So that's where this good comrade of ours came in." Michael motioned to the front the leader of the angelic military chorus.

As the angel strode forward, he commanded the attention of the hosts assembled. Without a nudge from the archangel, he boldly declared, "We all know that our Master deserves all praise!"

The sound of amens again shot through the ranks before him.

"But just how to offer it to Him under such peculiar circumstances? He is and was the King, yet He had cast off His royal robes for the mission. He came as a Prophet, but He could not yet utter a word. He came to be the High Priest of His people forever, yet He had not yet made the necessary passage to take up that role. So how to welcome Him?"

The other angles could feel the conundrum that had been set upon him.

"That is when we recalled that among all the other roles our Master came to fulfill, He promised to be the Good Shepherd. He had come in this way to seek and to save the lost sheep who had wandered from Him. So we concluded that there were none better to receive the news of His arrival and to join with us in uniting Heaven and earth in worshipping Him than earthly shepherds."

"They're not considered much by their own people. This, perhaps, is why our Master delights to take the role. It was the perfect disguise for His mission."

"And how did this go?" Michael prodded the angel along.

"Well, shepherds are mostly used to working alone. And these guys were the night shift, so they aren't used to many disturbances. So, I decided I'd go solo at first. I determined to show myself before I spoke. I just materialized before their eyes, and as the glory of the Lord shown around me, I realized I had their full attention. At that point, I cried out, 'Fear not, for behold, I bring you good news of great joy that will be for all the people. For unto you is born this day in the city of David a Savior, who is Christ the Lord. And this will be a sign for you: you will find a baby wrapped in swaddling cloths and lying in a manger.'"[85]

"And?" Michael prodded further.

"Well, before they had much chance to do or say anything, I brought in the whole crew."

With a sweep of the arm, he signaled his corps and a multitude of the assembled heavenly host fluttered their wings and rose slightly at the acknowledgement.

"We chose this as our song: 'Glory to God in the highest, and on earth peace among those with whom he is pleased!'"[86]

---

85   Luke 2:11
86   Luke 2:14

The mere sound of worship being offered to the Lord shot pulses of praise through the entire angelic throng, and they joined in intoning the words in unison with the commanding angel.

Michael let the praise linger in the air for a sweet moment. To honor their Creator was the joy of their hearts, and he didn't want to rob them of the pleasure in this moment before their greatest service to Him.

Unbeknownst to any of them, the commanding angel had slipped back among the host and left Michael at the fore. He recalled their theme and said, "There were other key angelic assignments in Jesus' first arrival. Not the least of which fell to this brother." Michael motioned a reluctant angel forward.

"Your assignment, my brother, was a particularly grievous one, was it not?"

All the angels knew the story and in anticipation of hearing it again cast their eyes downward.

The hesitant angel paused before beginning. "It was well after these events. The Magi had come from the east and had been redirected by the Master to find their way home by some route other than Jerusalem and the wicked Herod that it housed. But it didn't take Herod long to figure out what had happened. My orders came abruptly in the middle of the night. I was told that his murderous armies were doing double-time to reach Bethlehem."

Michael, aware of the sensitive nature of the events, asked, "Please continue, brother. What is it you were asked to do?"

"I was charged with getting Joseph, Mary, and the baby out of Bethlehem before Herod and his armies arrived. My orders were, above all else, to not let the evil one get a victory. A victory that would have, well . . ." His voice fell off.

"What strategy did you employ?"

"It was night. They were all asleep. So, I worked my way into Joseph's dream. I knew I had to make it terrifying enough to impress upon him the urgency of the situation and yet not so much as to paralyze him. I commanded him, 'Rise, take the child and his mother, and flee to Egypt, and remain there until I tell you, for Herod is about to search for the child, to destroy him.'"[87]

"His response?" Michael prodded.

"Oh, he got up, all right! It was a mad scramble, but they gathered their things and got just outside of town as the thundering hoofs of Herod's troops entered on the other side."

But then the angel's voice trailed off as he said in a choke of emotion, "And then . . ."

The angel looked downward in pain at the thought. Michael let the silence hang in the air as a testament to the tragedy that had then unfolded in Bethlehem.

"And then . . ." he tried again. Falling silent, he just shook his head in a pained remembrance.

Michael put a consoling arm upon the angel's shoulders and thanked him for his service and his report. The angel slipped back into the ranks from which he had come.

After a reflective moment or two, Michael carried the remaining narrative.

"And so our Master 'grew in wisdom and stature and in favor with God and man.'[88] Through the years of obscurity He, in reliance upon the Holy Spirit, trained Himself in the Father's Word. He

---

87   Matthew 2:13
88   Luke 2:52

nurtured His soul in the Father's presence through prayer. He labored alongside Joseph, crafting furniture, and making it a sacred art form. But eventually, the time came when He would stand to the fore. John began his preaching, calling the people to make ready the way for the Lord. Jesus, for His part, withdrew to the wilderness, where He neither ate nor drank for forty days. You know the epic battle that ensued as the evil one himself tried every tactic to cause our Master to fail. But He stood true. Then these, our brothers"—he motioned to a small band of angels to his left—"went to Him in the wilderness and, in His weakened physical state, nurtured Him back to strength."

Angels in every direction locked eyes with the small band of ministering spirits and nodded their affirmation.

Michael continued, "You know the hatred that stalked our Master at every turn. You know how it finally chased Him up upon the cross. You know how He suffered."

At the thought, soft sounds of mourning rose from the angels' ranks.

"You know how He loved."

They lifted their eyes upward in wondering amazement.

"You know how He died."

And with that, all Heaven fell silent. No one and nothing moved. No one spoke. It was their involuntary ritual of honor every time their Master's passion was openly mentioned.

Finally, Michael broke their contemplations, saying, "And you know the outcome."

The heels on angelic boots slapped in unison as myriads of myriads of angels came to attention at the mere thought of it!

"Jesus rose from the dead!" Michael shouted, his voice sounding the one note that always brought the angels to full, glorious frenzy. Cries, adulations, psalms, victory shouts arose in wave after wave of praise!

With outstretched arm, Michael's voice rose even further. "This chosen angel was honored to roll the stone away from His tomb to show the world the triumph of our King!"

The frenzy grew.

With a sweep of his other hand, he said, "These, our brothers, remained at the tomb to inform His followers of His triumph!"

The ringing report of swords slipping from sheaths filled the air. The entire heavenly host shone in a blinding recognition of the task that lay immediately before them, the brilliance of their reflected glory increasing by the moment.

Michael put the finishing touches upon these preparatory speeches by calling forward two especially large angels. Raising his voice above the din, he said, "You were there when the resurrected Jesus left earth, were you not?"

"We were," they reported with military snap.

"You lingered to instruct His disciples, did you not?"

"We did." They clipped their words again.

"And what is it you told them?"

"We asked, 'Men of Galilee, why do you stand looking into heaven?' Then we announced, 'This Jesus, who was taken up from you into heaven, will come in the same way as you saw him go into heaven.'"[89]

Then Michael cried to the entire assembled host, "And today is that day, my brothers in arms!"

---

89 Acts 1:11

They did not cry; they did not move; they did not shuffle nor clamor. Every angel in Heaven simply locked eyes with their commanding archangel, having readied themselves for the battle of the ages. This was their Master's moment—anticipated from before time began. They were about to put an end to all hostilities. Theirs was the assignment to join at their Master's side as He unveiled Himself in all His glory for every eye to see and for all the earth to marvel at Him. But before the peace that will never end can come, there is a battle to be waged.

Michael reviewed his troops, then shouted, "Final checks!"

He looked to his left and caught the attention of a division of angels. "Are you ready to gather all causes of sin and all lawbreakers?"

"Yes sir!" they shouted in unison.

He looked to his right and gathered in with his eyes another division. "Are you ready to gather from the four winds all the elect of God?"

"Yes sir!" came their reply.

With a sweep of his eyes, he took in the sight of Heaven's armies ordered and prepared. The sight of them all arrayed in fine linen, white and pure, and mounted upon their white horses would have stopped any but an angel's heart.

With that, Michael lifted his powerful right arm toward the throne, his sword triumphantly now overhead. He cried out a single command with a voice that reverberated through every atom of the created order: "*Ready!*"

At that, the sound of countless angels snapping to attention rang with crystal clarity through an otherwise-silent Heaven. Even the horses upon which they sat ceased their clawing at the clouds and fell still. All of Heaven's sentient beings set their eyes upon Michael and anticipated his next word of command. They had been waiting for this order for what seemed an eternity. Now it was just a word away. They watched as Michael inhaled deeply and opened his mouth. Angel hosts leaned forward in anticipation of the next sound they would hear.

And with that, the archangel let loose a cry of command that shot like a trumpet blast through the whole of creation.

And then in the next moment . . .

ACKNOWLEDGMENTS

THANK YOU, JESUS! YOU ARE the Center and Substance of the one great Story in which all our stories find context, meaning, and life.

Thank you, Julie! You always enjoy, affirm, and encourage my storytelling. Thanks for smiling and laughing.

Thank you, Melody, Joe, and Clint! You always demanded stories at bedtime. Thanks for making me believe you weren't just stalling.

Thank you, God! I taste Your pleasure when I tell Your Story.

SCRIPTURE INDEX

IF A STORY OR PORTION of a story has piqued your interest, you may wish to turn to the pertinent Scriptures for further reflection. The following passages are in some cases only alluded to and in others quoted precisely.

STAND UP AND BE COUNTED

Matthew 4:17

Luke 23:33

1 Corinthians 15:6

Matthew 28:11-15

Luke 9:22; 18:33

Luke 24:50-51; Acts 1:9-11

Acts 1:3, 8:12; 14:22; 19:8; 20:25; 28:23, 31

Luke 18:29-30

Isaiah 9:5

Luke 1:35; 22:70

Luke 19:10

Romans 5:6; 1 Peter 3:18

1 Corinthians 15:1-58

Romans 5:18; Galatians 3:28; Colossians 3:11

Romans 10:9-10

Matthew 3:2; Luke 13:3

Luke 9:23

Revelation 3:5; 13:8; 17:8; 20:12, 15; 21:27

Hebrews 9:27

Romans 3:24-25; 1 Peter 1:18-19

1 Timothy 6:15; Revelation 17:14; 19:16

Isaiah 45:23

Philippians 2:10-11

Romans 14:11

Daniel 7:27

Luke 9:23, 57-62

Philippians 2:10-11

Romans 14:11

Romans 10:9-10

Revelation 19:16

1 Peter 3:18

Revelation 1:18

John 3:16

Romans 12:1-2

Philippians 4:3

DELIVERY DAY

Exodus 1:15-22

Luke 2:1

Luke 2:7

Luke 2:4

Galatians 4:4

Matthew 1:21-25; Luke 1:31; 2:21

Matthew 1:20-21

Luke 1:31

Luke 2:8-20

Luke 2:21

Matthew 1:21

Luke 2:22-24

Matthew 2:11

Isaiah 59:20-21

Romans 11:26-27

Matthew 2:1-12

Matthew 2:13-18

Matthew 2:19-23

Luke 7:11-17

Matthew 22:15-22; Mark 12:13-17; Luke 20:19-26

Mark 12:41-44; Luke 21:1-4

Matthew 26:47-56; Mark 14:43-52; Luke 22:47-53; John 18:2-12

John 19:4-5, 12

John 19:15

Matthew 27:33-35; Mark 15:22-24; Luke 23:33; John 19:17-18

Matthew 27:39-44; Mark 15:29-32; Luke 23:35-37; John 19:25-27

Luke 23:34

Matthew 2:16-18

Isaiah 53:3-12

John 19:30

Matthew 28:1-8; Mark 16:1-11; Luke 24:1-11; John 20:1-18

Mark 16:12-13; Luke 24:13-35

Isaiah 59:20-21

Romans 11:26-27

The Lost Shepherd

Matthew 18:12-13; Luke 15:4-7

Luke 2:20

Matthew 9:36; Mark 6:34

Luke 15:4-5

Luke 19:10

John 10:1-30

John 10:11, 14

John 10:27

John 10:3

Luke 2:8-20

Matthew 2:13-15

Luke 2:22-24

Luke 2:11

Luke 2:7

Matthew 1:16, 18-25; Luke 1:27; 2:4, 16

Matthew 13:55; Mark 6:3

Luke 2:39

John 1:46

Micah 5:2; Matthew 2:6

Matthew 1:21, 25; Luke 1:31; 2:21

Matthew 27:33; Mark 15:22; John 19:17

Matthew 27:45; Mark 15:33; Luke 23:44

Isaiah 53:6

John 10:11

Luke 19:10

Luke 15:4-5

Isaiah 53:7; Acts 8:32

Matthew 28:1-10; Mark 16:1-13; Luke 24:1-49; John 20:1-23

Matthew 28:11-15

1 Corinthians 15:6

John 10:14

John 10:1-10

Matthew 28:20

THE WEIGHT OF WAITING

Luke 2:29-32

Luke 2:35

The Scribe Who Must Be Right

Deuteronomy 6:1-9

Mark 12:38; Luke 20:46

Matthew 23:6; Mark 12:39-40; Luke 11:43; 20:46-47

Micah 5:1-6

Matthew 2:3-4

Matthew 2:1-3

Micah 5:2

Matthew 2:6

Matthew 2:16-23

Jeremiah 38:15

Matthew 2:13-15

Hosea 11:1

Matthew 2:15

Luke 2:41-52

Psalm 8:2

John 1:46

Matthew 7:29; 21:23

Mark 12:28-33

Mark 12:34

Luke 20:39-47

Matthew 23:2

Acts 3:22; 7:37

Deuteronomy 18:15, 18

Matthew 26:47-27:1; Mark 14:43-15:1; Luke 22:47-71; John 18:2-24

Isaiah 53:10-11

Psalm 143:2

Matthew 27:31-34; Mark 15:20-23; Luke 23:26-33; John 19:17

Isaiah 52:14

Matthew 13:52

Isaiah 53:3

Isaiah 53:5

Matthew 27:42; Mark 15:31; Luke 23:35

Luke 23:34

Isaiah 53:8

Luke 23:43

Isaiah 53:9

Psalm 22:1; Matthew 27:46; Mark 15:34

John 19:30

Isaiah 53:10

Luke 23:46

Matthew 27:50; Mark 15:37; Luke 23:46; John 19:30

Isaiah 53:11

Romans 1:16-17; 3:21-26; Galatians 2:15-16; Colossians 3:9-10

1 Corinthians 1:19-25

CUSTOM-MADE

Jeremiah 43:13; Isaiah 19:18

Acts 8:27

Acts 8:26-40

Acts 8:30-33

Isaiah 53:7-8

Acts 8:34-35

John 1:1, 14

Matthew 5:17

Isaiah 52:13-53:12

Acts 5:31

Romans 3:21-26; 6:6, 22

Matthew 28:6; Mark 16:6; Luke 24:6

1 Corinthians 15:3-6

Acts 1:6-11

Ecclesiastes 3:11

Acts 8:36-40

Matthew 2:13-15

Matthew 1:18-25; Luke 1:26-38

Matthew 120-21, 25

Luke 1:31; 2:21

Luke 2:1-7

Matthew 2:13-18

Acts 8:26-40

Matthew 1:18-2:18; Luke 1:26-66; 2:1-21

John 1:1, 14

Acts 5:31

Romans 3:21-26

1 Corinthians 15:3-6

Acts 1:6-11

Acts 2:1-41

Jeremiah 13:23

2 Corinthians 5:17

John 3:1-15

Genesis 37-50

Genesis 41:45, 50; 46:20

Isaiah 19:18-21

Isaiah 19:22, 25

Mark 6:3

John 6:44

Romans 8:28; 9:24; 1 Thessalonians 2:12; 1 Peter 5:10

Mark 6:3

Malachi 4:2

Ephesians 3:14-19

Romans 16:25-27

ADVENT ARMIES

Luke 1:13-17

Luke 1:20

Luke 1:28

Luke 1:30

Luke 1:31-33

Luke 1:37

Luke 1:38

Matthew 1:20

Matthew 1:21; Luke 1:31

Luke 2:11

Luke 2:14

Matthew 2:13-14

Luke 2:52

Acts 1:11

IS BIBLICAL HISTORICAL FICTION *BIBLICAL*?

WHAT ARE WE TO MAKE of this matter of *biblical* fiction? What about taking Bible narratives and reimagining them, inserting additional characters, adding background "color," filling in dramatic detail to impress the *feel* of the story even more deeply upon the reader? In short, what about expanding upon the stories of the Bible? Is there any biblical warrant for doing so?

Or, in this pursuit, does one automatically become guilty of adding to Scripture (Deut. 4:2; 1 Cor. 4:6; Rev. 22:18) and thereby incur the curses inherent in doing so?

Let's seek an answer first by examining another way of handling the text of Scripture, including its narrative portions. Consider preaching. What is it the preacher does when he speaks at length on any given narrative within the canon of Scripture? Does not the expositor "add" to Scripture when he unpacks, explains, or expands upon what the author meant and intended as guided by the Holy Spirit? He certainly adds words to it! The average preacher takes a good deal longer to unpack a passage of Scripture than it would take simply to read it.

But this is not sin, is it? Isn't this exactly what the Scriptures themselves call for? For "the unfolding of your words gives light" (Psalm 119:130a)!

In the case of preaching, this "unfolding" is accomplished through *explanation*; but what of doing so via *imagination*?

Does imagination necessarily violate the integrity of the scriptural text? If explanation and exhortation can unfold the Divine intent behind a passage of Scripture, is it possible that an imaginative retelling of the narrative might achieve this as well?

I believe this is possible. But this, of necessity, becomes a special kind of imaginative retelling. In this sense, *biblical* fiction is not precisely like other works of historical fiction. The author of historical fiction may feel free to imprint the record of history with his desired angle on things. Historians may call him to account, but sometimes, this is because they disagree with his "take" on history. The author's take is not their take.

But in the case of *biblical* fiction, the storyteller must answer to the Author of all things. The storyteller must discover what the original Storyteller intended when He breathed out the inspired words of the scriptural account. The storyteller must make his/her story serve that intent.

But perhaps we are getting ahead of ourselves. Let's establish a basic ground rule for those writing biblical historical fiction. We must agree that, as the adage goes, all history is His Story. God is sovereign Lord of all that occurs. So, in this light, the work of history itself is a sacred undertaking. Thus, at one level, the writer of historical fiction faces the same issues that we raise here about *biblical* fiction.

Though this is true, we should also note that biblical fiction faces the additional blessing/burden that, in this case, God Himself has given us the record of this particular slice of history. We possess His very words conveying His Sovereign and completely accurate and sufficient rendering of the Story and all the stories it contains. Our storytelling and all that goes with it (such as imagination, character creation, inventive dialogue, etc.) must conform to the purpose for which God Himself told the scriptural story. We may use more words (just as a preacher does), but our words must serve to unfold the words God chose to tell the original story.

The author of *biblical* fiction, just like the preacher of God's Word, must submit him/herself to the text of Scripture and the God Who breathed it out, seeking to serve Him and His original purposes for the accounts.

Some might complain that this unnecessarily squelches the author's creativity. I think, rather, it heightens the powerful possibilities of his/her story! For now, we are not simply working with what our words might produce, but what the unleashing of God's Word might bring forth. And we all know the Big Story, the Original Story, the True Story, the Real Story began with, "And God said . . ." (Gen. 1:3, 6, 9, 11, 14, 20, 24, 26).

The peculiar joy of the author of *biblical* fiction (as with any Bible preacher worth his salt) is to realize that one has somehow joined God in what He is doing and unfolded His Word; and as a result, light has come to one's readers. Light that gives Life. Light and Life that the Creator Himself says is "very good" (Gen. 1:31).

But, you ask, do we have any scriptural *example* of this kind of thing?

It's a great question. An example, in one sense, is difficult to provide because you're asking whether Scripture does to itself what we are considering a contemporary author doing with Scripture. Under that guise, finding an example seems unlikely.

But upon further consideration, I think we may have at least a near-example of this very kind of thing.

Remember when David was unfaithful with Bathsheba? When he was unable to cover his act by manipulating her husband, he saw to it that he was killed in battle. The child was born; David married Bathsheba.

End of story, right?

Not exactly. In fact, it was the birth of a new, divinely fictionalized story.

God sent the prophet Nathan to reimagine the facts of David's story in order to get around his defenses and bring conviction over and confession of his sin. Nathan came to David to recount a story—which he passed off as true to fact—of power, abuse, and murder. Only in this case, it didn't involve a king, a faithful servant, and his wife. Instead, it retells David's story (2 Sam. 11) through a fictional tale of a poor man, his pet lamb, and his rich and powerful neighbor (2 Sam. 12:1-6).

This fictional tale of David's sin was powerfully used of God to bring the king to repentance (2 Sam. 12:7-15).

Consider other possible examples. Remember how Ezekiel, under the inspiration of the Holy Spirit, tells the past story of Israel and Judah by way of stories about an abandoned infant who becomes a faithless bride (Ezek. 16), two eagles and three shoots of a cedar tree (Ezek. 17), and two young women named Oholah and Oholibah (Ezek. 23). And some of these stories ought to be rated at least PG-13!

Neither the scriptural narrative of Nathan's fictionalized story about David's sin nor Ezekiel's imaginative retelling of the history of God's people *prescribe* reimagining and retelling of the historical story for ministry purposes. But could we say that they *permit* it? Perhaps even *invite* it?

Nathan's and Ezekiel's stories were divinely affirmed when God included them in the inspired text of Scripture. Our imaginative recounting of biblical history won't (and shouldn't) be affirmed in this way. But we can pray that God might be pleased to use our fictionalized renderings of biblical, historical events to similarly change the lives of readers for eternity. Such life-transformation by the power of the Holy Spirit is the one Divine affirmation for which every Christian writer longs.

ABOUT THE AUTHOR

JOHN KITCHEN GREW UP ON the plains of rural Iowa, part of a good but unbelieving family. God saved his entire family from a near-fatal asphyxiation accident when John was a child. This put in motion a series of events that led to John's conversion as an adolescent. Later, he answered God's call to vocational service and began pastoral ministry in 1987. He and his wife, Julie, currently serve an international church in the Middle East. They have three adult children, two beautiful daughters-in-law, and an amazing granddaughter. John is the author of over a dozen books. This is his first work of fiction.

CONTACT INFORMATION

You can follow John at www.jkitchen.org. There you will find more content and information on how you can contact him. John would love to hear how God has used this book in your life.

Ambassador International's mission is to magnify the Lord Jesus Christ and promote His Gospel through the written word.

We believe through the publication of Christian literature, Jesus Christ and His Word will be exalted, believers will be strengthened in their walk with Him, and the lost will be directed to Jesus Christ as the only way of salvation.

For more information about
AMBASSADOR INTERNATIONAL
please visit:

www.ambassador-international.com
@AmbassadorIntl
www.facebook.com/AmbassadorIntl

Thank you for reading, and please consider leaving us a review on Amazon, Goodreads, or our websites.

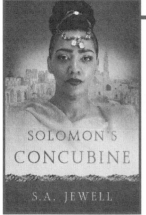

King Solomon is well-known as a wise man and the wealthiest king to have ever lived. But with great power often comes great corruption, and Solomon was no exception—including his collection of wives and concubines. But who were these women? What was life like for them in Solomon's harem? S.A. Jewell dives into a deeper part of Solomon's kingdom and shows how God is always faithful, even when we may doubt His plan.

Daniel was just a teenager when he was taken captive by the Babylonians, never to see his family again. As Daniel and his friends strive to make the best of their circumstances—slaves in the king's court—they also fight to honor their vows to the one true God amidst a people who worship only false gods. From slave to the highest position in the king's court, Daniel shows how God can use an ordinary person to do extraordinary things.

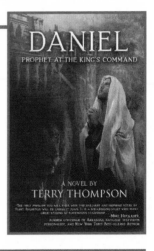

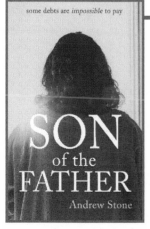

Long before his life is traded for Jesus', Barabbas' family is ruined, a consequence of his own rage. Consumed with guilt he resolves to put things right, but this seems an impossible task as huge debts, revenge, theft, and murder hang above his head. As Barabbas struggles to atone and restore his family's honor, he meets the new religious teacher. Barabbas can't bring himself to trust this wandering preacher until Barabbas' life is spared, costing more than he thought possible.

Made in the USA
Las Vegas, NV
13 December 2022